Hopeless Romantic

By Mansi Jikadara B.

FROG BOOKS

First published in India 2015 by Frog Books
An imprint of Leadstart Publishing Pvt Ltd
1 Level, Trade Centre
Bandra Kurla Complex
Bandra (East) Mumbai 400 051 India
Telephone: +91-22-40700804
Fax: +91-22-40700800
Email: info@leadstartcorp.com
www.leadstartcorp.com / www.frogbooks.net

Sales Office:
Unit No.25/26, Building No.A/1,
Near Wadala RTO,
Wadala (East), Mumbai – 400037 India
Phone: +91 22 24046887

US Office:
Axis Corp, 7845 E Oakbrook Circle
Madison, WI 53717 USA

ISBN 978-93-84027-68-1
Book Editor: Surojit Mohan Gupta
Design Editor: Mishta Roy
Layout: Logiciels Info Solutions Pvt. Ltd.

Typeset in Book Antiqua
Printed at Dhote Offset Technokrafts Pvt. Ltd., Mumbai

Price — India: Rs 199

Dedication

To the Man I love the most.

Dear Daddy,

Thank you for being such a wonderful father to me. I miss you more each day and come what may, I'll always be your little girl.

About the Author

Mansi Jikadara B. is a Unicorn disguised in a human body. She tried her hand at writing at the age of seventeen and Hopeless Romantic is her very first novel. Apart from her interest in writing she also loves painting, sketching, paper art and sometimes cooking. If not a writer she'd definitely be a vampire! She also writes poetry, to read the #TypewriterDaily Poetry Series — you can check out:

Instagram: www.instagram.com/poet_withatypewriter/
Facebook page: www.facebook.com/PoetWithATypewriter/
Blogs: http://thetypewriterdaily.tumblr.com
Twitter: https://twitter.com/WordWeaver5

Acknowledgements

Big, big heartfelt thanks to my mother, for always supporting me. My sister Nisha and her husband, Puran, for helping me write and rewrite this novel. My best friend, Mili Radia, for always listening to my pointless drama. Priyanka Joshi, Mansi Joshi and Gunjan Kotak for always being there for me—you guys rock! I would also like to thank Rael Sanchis, Krutika Hindocha, Jannelle Britto, Manali Jain, Thomson Fernandes, Aditya Shastri, Jill Radia, Virali Panchamia, Urmi Panchamia, Shreya Modi, Aman Sheth and Himanshu Chhabra—for bringing a smile on my face and making me a better person. Also, the entire team of Leadstart Publishing, for being so supportive and guiding me throughout the journey!

Because Love, only Love can complete us.

Contents

How beautiful it is to lose yourself in someone—
and not feel lost at the same time.

~ Mansi

Chapter 1

"Honey, why are you wearing the T-shirt inside out?" Dad remarks, the moment I enter the kitchen. I immediately check the T-shirt not once, but twice.

"Dad!" I yell I am already going mad thinking about tomorrow, but my Dad doesn't leave a chance to mock me down during such situations.

"All set for tomorrow?" He questions me, putting a spoon full of chocolate fudge cake in his mouth, staring at the remaining slice.

"Yeah," I lie, opening the refrigerator.

"Then, why are you up in the middle of the night, honey?" He adds, eyeing me suspiciously.

"Well, why are you up?" I reply smartly, pouring some milk in a glass and sit beside him.

"As far as I am pointed to that question well, I felt this last slice of cake seemed lonely back in the refrigerator, so you better tell me what's wrong?" He questions, curiously.

"I am hungry." I answer lying again, drinking some milk from the glass.

"Seriously, you really want me to believe that?" He argues, putting a piece of fudge cake in my mouth.

"It's too sweet." I complain, wiping the chocolate away from my lips.

"Nervous?" He questions, yet again.

"Umm, a little," I respond smiling, trying hard to hide my nervousness, which kept haunting me in my room and resulted in bringing me into the kitchen. I have a peculiar habit of eating something whenever I am nervous, but unfortunately I've had a heavy dinner so today I am just going to stick to milk.

"Mmmm," he mumbles, cutting the remaining slice into two.

"Honey, you know, you're not good at hiding stuff," he remarks, looking me in the eye.

"Dad, I am just a little nervous and restless. That's it!" I explain to him, finishing the milk.

"Everything's going to be fine; just give time, a little time," he assures.

"Okay, night Dad." I wish him goodnight and start walking back to my room. How can he be so calm about all of this, how?

William Dalton, my Dad, is a lawyer. We are more like best friends than a 'typical' father and daughter type. He means everything to me and I mean the world to him though he tells me that, one day my prince charming will find me and then he'll be all alone. But the way I am, I think there are no chances of any prince charming arriving for me. What I mean to say is that I am a complete recluse and my father on the other hand is crazy, like literally crazy! We are completely different; I think I am more like my Mum, but only if I'd known her. I never really got a chance to know her. All I know is that they both, Mum and Dad got married at a very young age. Grandma met my Mum, Rebecca, in one of their gatherings and she pretty much liked her. Dad on the other hand, couldn't say a no and besides Mum and Dad got along well together. After a year and a half I entered their life. I was a month old when my Mum met with an accident and couldn't make it through. That's the sad part of the story, but eventually my Dad moved on and now he has a girlfriend. There's this funny story behind naming me he told me once. My Dad was busy with a meeting when Mum was taken to the hospital. Once, the process was over and I was safely born into this world, Mum had a little argument with him on not being there for me. So, my Dad promised my Mum that I'd be his most important 'case' henceforth and my Mom added a 'y' to it, that's how I came to be named, 'CASEY' and that's the only thing I know about Mum, we never ever discussed anything about Mum. Never. And besides when I see my Dad happy and finally moving on with someone who is genuinely nice, I don't feel like bringing the past between the both of them and I am sure that Mum too would be happy with all of this.

******

"This whole new-school thing is freaking me out," I exclaim, analyzing myself in the mirror. My mind is exhausted totally, thinking about the new school, talking to Dad didn't help either. How can I be all calm and composed when I am joining the school right in the mid-term? The thought itself is so scary, let alone the syllabus that I may have to cope up with. I lay in my bed consumed with all these eerie thoughts. Well, I know it sounds bizarre but yes; I am not prepared for my new school. Remember, that sick feeling you feel down in your stomach when we had to go to the school at the age of 5, yes; exactly that is what I am feeling. This is the third time I am readjusting my life because of Dad's transfer, this time it's Chicago. I've been here in my childhood, but the memory is completely blurred and Chicago too seems different from what I remember. I was seven when I'd accompanied Dad for one of his meetings. It was a short two days and one night trip, but since my father was busy with his clients, I was strictly not allowed to leave the hotel. Although Chicago looks beautiful at night, but maybe it's just more developed now. Back in New York I have had an anti-social life, just a couple of friends (Three actually; Susan, Susan's boyfriend Daniel and my Dad) and a normal routine life so shifting doesn't really affect me in a way, but going to a new school and meeting a whole lot of people do. Besides that, I can't let him on his own, that's not me. He has always been there for me since forever and now it is time to return him the favour. But this is not what I am worried about; I am worried because I am *me*. I would be the only person on earth who would be afraid of making new friends or go on adventures and do all those things that the people my age would love to do, not only that, but I also think that I make people feel awkward around myself or maybe just don't connect with them, so you can say that I am pretty much inhuman.

"It's not your mistake Casey; you are just not good enough at expressing yourself, sweetie." Susan's voice keeps ringing in my ears. Susan Martin, she is the only friend I've ever had after I understood the concept of friend. I still can't find the reason behind she being friends with me; I mean who would ever befriend me? I am a junk!

I hope everything turns out well tomorrow and I hope it would be a start of something new; a new beginning.

******

I have no idea about how I fell asleep last night, but the alarm helped me wake up, at the right time. After saying a short prayer I walk to the washroom and start brushing my teeth. While wiping my face, I hear Dad knocking my bedroom door.

"Case...Case,"

"Morning, Dad!" I say, opening the door.

"Morning honey, the breakfast is all ready, waiting for you down at the table. I have to leave early today as I have a meeting," he explains, giving a peck on my forehead.

"Okay," I reply, giving him a peck on his cheek.

"And yeah, good luck for your new school," he adds, smiling.

I smile and wave him goodbye from the window as I see him get inside his car. So, now it is just me in this big, 2 storey apartment. Soon after my mind accepts that I am all alone, the nervousness starts creeping up on me. I freshen myself up, use my favourite shampoo and try hard to think nothing, but the more I try to escape the thoughts the more they keep coming back. So, I decide to chant these words, "Everything is perfect." While having my breakfast I see a note written by Dad on the refrigerator.

"Make some new friends (boyfriend) Have fun. Love you!"

I stare at the word boyfriend for a few seconds until I hear my phone ringing, I am sure it is Susan.

"I am so damn nervous," I complain on receiving the call.

"Casey, relax," she orders, from the other end.

"I can't. You know what sort of person I am ... such a..." Before I complete she interrupts.

"You're a sweetheart."

"Whatever," I mutter, rolling my eyes.

"Case, you are really a wonderful person. Stop underestimating yourself, you're different from others but that's what makes you, you." She explains, shouting a little.

"It's difficult for me Susan," I murmur.

"I know but just trust your-self a little bit," she says, consoling.

"I will try." That's the only thing I reply.

"And if you find a cute or maybe a hot guy, please talk to him. Anybody would find you cute," she adds.

"Susan!" I exclaim.

"What, you are not a child anymore," she argues.

"I am not ready Susan. I just can't." I explain.

"What do you mean by that? I am not telling you to straight away sleep with him!" She argues shouting a little

"Susan, you know what exactly I meant. And guys do not fall in love with girls like me," I remark.

"Case, you're exactly the kind of a girl guy fall in love with." She shouts again and hangs up.

God knows why she wants me to forcefully fall in love with someone. Back in school, she tried a lot of times to hook me up with every guy she thought would like me, but nothing ever worked out. Susan has a boyfriend and they both are just made for each other, but that doesn't mean she would get her best friend hooked up with any random guy because she wants me to know what love feels like. It really sounds lame. I know it feels good to be with someone; someone you love. But I am not going to look around everywhere for him. Never. A moment later, I hear my phone beep, it is Susan. I open the text message:

Good luck! I am sorry :(

I quickly type a text: *Thanks and I will talk but only if the guy seems cute! :)*

She responds: *also if he is Hot! :p*

I reply: *Stop it now! I will let you know about it after school. Love you...Take care.*

She says: *desperately waiting! :)*

I have enough of time to get ready and reach school. So after having my breakfast and getting tips from my best friend, who is also my only friend, I come to my room and remove my favourite blouse with the other stuff. I put the iron on and get into my pants. As soon as, I keep the iron on the blouse the telephone rings and I run downstairs.

"Hello," I say, holding my breath.

"Samantha, why have you not been answering my calls?? I know there is something wrong between you and Phil," an old lady shouts, from the other side.

"Ma'am, I guess there's a mistake; this is the Dalton residence and there is no, Samantha neither Phil here," I calmly explain to her and disconnect the line.

I come upstairs and then the sight in front of my eyes multiplies my nervousness. The chanting isn't working anymore.

"Nothing is perfect," I mutter under my breath.

My blouse is all burned and there is a huge hole formed in between because I kept that bloody iron over it and rushed to receive the call, I ruined everything! The next moment I panic, I remove everything from my closet, totally confused about what to wear. After going through almost everything I finally end up with a black full sleeves sweatshirt with purple prints on it. I tie my hair into a pony, one last glance in the mirror and I can say I manage to look good somehow. I take my bag; check everything twice before closing the door and leave in my car for my new school "Franklin High."

My heartbeats are racing and the same feeling starts knocking me down again. I keep murmuring to myself 'it is okay Casey, it's just a new school … just be calm'. The more I get closer the more I am getting nervous. I park the car in the parking lot, get out of it, take a deep breath and order myself, "Relax". Franklin High has a lot of buildings, just like my old school, but it also has a huge playground and lots of trees around it. I start walking to the office, observing around. There are groups of students, some laughing, some busy reading stuff, some fighting and some couples holding hands and kissing each other; suddenly, I start hearing whispers most of them are male voices. I try hard to ignore them, but they are still audible, "she's cute" "Is she a newbie...?" "I'll ask her out for prom." "Dude you can't because Jason..." and the voices trail off after I enter the office, once the door gets locked up.

"Excuse me; I am Casey ... Casey Dalton." I introduce myself to the office representative. She is in her forties; the wrinkles beneath her grey eyes are visible through her thick glass frame. She smiles apologetically searching for something on her desk and simultaneously talks over the phone.

"Welcome Casey, here's your schedule ... have a good day." She finally hands me my schedule, keeping the phone aside.

"You too," I smile taking my schedule and head outside.

I walk out of the office with my head inside the schedule. I see that the first class is Algebra and it's in building 2, opposite to the gym ... and there I create another Mess!!

"I am really sorry... I just ... uhh," I apologize, helping the girl collect her books which are scattered over the floor because I'd bumped into her while I was trying to read my schedule.

"That's okay," she responds instantly.

"Hey, I am Stella, Stella Simon." She introduces herself, smiling.

"Hi, I am Case... Casey Dalton," I manage to reply, trying my best to not sound stupid or make her feel awkward.

"So you're the newbie, every guy is talking about," she adds, her eyes widening a little as she studies me.

"Umm... I have no idea..."

"Joking ... so which is your first class?" She cuts me midway.

"Algebra," I say, recollecting in my mind.

"Mine too!" She says cheerfully.

In the back of my mind it goes, "5 minutes in the new school and already a friend, not bad Case." My new friend Stella Simon seems a little girlish; curly hair, pink bag which has a keychain in heart shape, a bracelet and a little gloss on her lips. I find her cute on the other hand; chirpy voice, small nose and almond eyes. We both head towards our first class; Algebra. She settles on the chair next to mine and exchanges some words with the girl on her right side. I am about to dig myself in the textbook, when she questions me,

"You know anybody here?"

"Not really, my Dad and I moved here because of his transfer," I explain, fidgeting with the pages of the book.

"And what about your Mom?" she adds, observing the pages and that very moment I close the book shut.

"Uhh... I lost her when I was a month old, but you never know she can be here; right in this classroom, watching over both of us," I explain, smiling and hoping that she wouldn't stretch this topic. She smiles and I notice a tinge of pain touching her eyes, as the smile widens.

"Well, then don't you dare flirt with any of the guys because your Mom can scare the shit out of them," she adds, laughing.

"Yeah," I reply, imagining about it.

"Boyfriend?" she asks, typing something in her cell phone.

I am about to answer, but our Algebra teacher enters the class.

Mr Anderson takes our attendance and starts with the syllabus. He solves a few sums and allots a few for homework. I am trying to solve the first sum allotted for homework when I hear Mr Anderson's voice.

"Casey Dalton, are we doing well?" he questions, smiling a warm smile.

"Yes," I reply smiling awkwardly. I feel 110 eyes gaping at me, so I bury myself inside the book.

The class goes off well and everybody here seems friendly except some people who keep staring at me unnecessarily.

"Which is your next class?" Stella questions me.

"Social Studies," I reply, looking into the schedule.

"It's in building 3," I add, as I observe her eyes searching for something in my schedule.

"Building 3, take the stairs down and then take right, okay?" she explains giving the directions.

"Okay," I reply, smiling.

"Meet you in the break," she says and waves me goodbye.

I walk in the direction of the class, smiling. I am happy that everything is falling into place. Chanting the "everything is perfect" mantra actually worked. I enter the class and settle in the second row, the first chair from the right. I patiently wait for the teacher to arrive.

"Casey Dalton." I hear a guy calling out my name, who I think is probably sitting behind me.

I turn around and find a cute geek boy, smiling at me.

"Hi," I say, smiling. He smiles back wider and my eyes see the braces underneath, short black curly noodle hair and tiny eyes, which are covered under the black framed thick glasses.

"I am Ethan Clarkson," he adds.

"Nice to meet you," I reply and turn around as the teacher enters the class.

Mr Andrews explains the syllabus for the test which is going to be held in the next week. We quickly jot down the notes and then he continues with the syllabus. Once he is over with today's class, I start packing my bag. I am about to keep my pencil in my bag, but unfortunately it slips out of my hand, I move my hand down to pick it up, but by then Ethan already picks it up for me.

"Thanks," I say, taking it from him.

He smiles yet again and thank God, at the same time the bell rings. I carefully keep the pencil and the book in my bag not that I am afraid it may fall again, but I just don't want Ethan to help me with that. It's awkward and he seems too shy! I check my schedule for the next class, it is Biology. The thought itself makes me sleepy. I bid Ethan goodbye and climb upstairs because the class is in the same building on the third floor. I check the name of the teacher in the schedule; Mr Mathews. Well, aren't there any female teachers in the school or any cute male teacher would also do. I walk to the class and sit on the second last chair; I have a habit of dozing off in the Bio class. Bio lecture doesn't make me sleep. Actually it keeps me alarmed, there is this guy sitting two chairs away from me and I have no idea why, but all this while he's just staring at me. God, it is so damn embarrassing, for a while I feel I am naked. It is as if his eyes are glued to me. Thankfully, the class ends and I immediately walk to Stella, as I see her waiting outside the class.

"So ... how's it going??" she asks.

"Umm ... horrible." I reply, rolling my eyes.

"I don't think Franklin High is that bad," she remarks.

"Not the school ... the boys. I mean they watch me as if I am an alien or I am naked or something..." I try to explain.

"Well, that they would do because they find you interesting!" she says, rolling her eyes and smiling naughtily.

I have no idea what to say, so I just keep mum. And secondly WHY DO THEY FIND ME INTERESTING?

"You know what Casey ... you're kind of different," I hear her say.

"Like what??" I ask, trying to understand.

"Generally, girls try to get attention and you are the complete opposite of that," she reasons.

"I don't know I just feel awkward..." Before I complete we are surrounded by a couple of people.

"Casey this is Mark, Jessica and he is Zac." She introduces the people around us.

"Hi," I say, making a hand gesture. Jessica looks beautiful and Mark is kind of the boy next door who keeps holding Jessica's hand all the time which also means they are together. Both look adorable. For a split second Susan and her boyfriend Daniel's picture flashes in front of my eyes. Zac reminds me of someone, but I can't remember whom; he has features which are similar to those bad boys. Great physique, short military hair and a tattoo in some alien language on his left arm.

"How's it going?" Jessica questions me.

"Nice, I didn't expect to make so many friends on day one," I respond, smiling and trying to believe that I did make a lot of friends.

"Hungry?" Stella interrupts, keeping the cell phone in her pocket.

"Starving," I respond and we walk towards the food section. I take a cheese sandwich, orange juice and French fries.

"Case, you are gonna become fat if you keep eating junk." Stella mocks.

"Well, I don't think so, lack of fat muscles." I say, smiling an evil grin.

"Lucky you," she replies and we walk back to our table. I quickly eat my lunch listening to their conversations which has baseball practice, science project trip, and Jessica's health issues and lastly it shifts to Prom. I am sipping the juice down my mouth when Jessica changes the discussions to the Prom night asking something to Mark. It almost makes me choke a little, I am not good at dancing and things like Prom nights make me feel claustrophobic. Thank God, that the bell rings at the same time and we all head towards our respective classes.

"Which is your next class?" Stella questions me. She is so similar to Susan. I am sure if I mention Stella to Susan she will be jealous as hell.

"Literature," I answer with a smile, as I remember the schedule.

"Okay, meet you after school then," she says and bids me goodbye.

******

I walk to the Literature class checking the teacher's name in the schedule. I assemble myself on the third chair in the second row, waiting for this and the next class, Chemistry, to gets over ASAP. I am so sleepy after loading my stomach with a cheese sandwich I can hardly keep my eyes open. Finally she arrives, the first female teacher. Mrs Clark looks average with blonde hair, medium height; say around 5 feet 3 inch and blue-ish eyes. She explains to us about the extract, which she is about to show in today's class, and switches on the presentation. The lights get dim and I am tuned off from reality to my own world. I close my eyes and open them again, recollecting the entire day. Well, the day went beyond my expectations and it was surprising for me that I had made so many friends in so little time. But in spite of all this, something seems missing. I can't figure out what it is, but I am sure that something is either missing or there is something I am forgetting maybe...

The bell rings and the lights are switched on, transporting me to reality. "I need to keep my thoughts away in the class," I mutter under my breath. I am hardly attentive in the class, this is so not done. Besides this, I am happy that there is just one class left; Chemistry. I head in the direction of the lab, trying to tighten the rubber band in my hair. I keep walking, holding books in one hand while the other hand works on the rubber band. I am a step away from entering the lab but *BANG*. I have no idea how, but I just tripped off, while securing the rubber band in place.

"I am such a mess," I mutter under my breath and start collecting the books which are scattered around the floor when I notice another hand around mine. He looks up at me, his perfect pink lips, which a second later, opens into a beautiful warm smile, makes my heart melt. I try to smile but I just can't. I am so fascinated by him. As I watch him like a star-struck fan, he jerks his head slightly making his golden-ish black hair fall over his dark emerald eyes, framed by black eyelashes. His nose so str...

"Here," he disturbs my thoughts and hands over the book to me.

"Thanks," I somehow manage to reply.

"All cool, Casey?" he adds. In the back of my mind it goes, HE.KNOWS.MY.NAME.

"Yeah," I say, smiling like an idiot.

"Hi, I am Jason Ellwood," he says, moving his hand forward. His hand seems strong with some veins visible, long fingers and nails have a tinge of pinkness and just when I am about to touch him, all the students start moving inside the lab. He immediately shakes his hand down and signals me to walk inside.

"If only I'd stopped admiring his hand, I would have possibly touched him!" I wonder to myself.

Chapter 2

Mr Smith, our Chemistry teacher enters the lab and shoots a stern look at Jason.

"Attention everyone, we have a new student Casey Dalton joining the school this year. I am sure all of you would welcome her warmly," he says, looking at me and then at everyone.

I smile blankly and everyone in the lab smiles back at me. I walk to the only empty section visible in the class. I quickly settle myself and remove my journal. I glance ahead towards Mr Smith and Jason; they are discussing something. Seems like Jason is convincing Mr Smith and he seems completely unconvinced by him. A moment later, I feel everybody's eyes on me and so without looking around I peep inside the journal. My heartbeat increases and I try to look around from the corner of my eye. I see someone walking towards my seat, the shoes seem familiar. It's him; Jason. In a matter of seconds he is sitting beside me. I force myself to look at him; I mean I can't ignore him. It is impossible! He looks at me and then looks away. I find myself staring at him and immediately turn back to my journal as I realize that.

"Hi, again," I hear him say.

His voice makes me more nervous, I hear my heart throbbing clearly. I purse my lips and try to act normal.

"Hi," I reply, smiling a little.

"So, do you like Chemistry?" he questions smiling.

"Yeah, it's my favourite subject," I answer, looking at the journal and then at him.

In the meanwhile, Mr Smith starts with the class and talks something about the diffusion of solids into err ... something. I am not sure for the first time. How can anyone in the world concentrate when you have someone like him sitting beside you?? I watch him from the corner of my eyes, he seems so chilled out and I on the other hand feel completely opposite of it.

"I am your partner in the Chemistry project," he informs, looking straight into my eyes.

I blink twice and try to process the meaning of his words. I am awestruck in his presence. The moment his words make sense my heart dances in amusement. I am like, Yay!

"What is the project about?" I question acting all cool and hiding my happiness.

He smiles a little too much and then answers, "I really don't know."

I nod back smiling awkwardly. He sure is thinking that I don't like him, but the truth is he is so damn innocent, cute, hot, gorgeous, sexy, and I need to Google more adjectives, as I am running out of words to describe him.

"We need to ask Mr Smith after the class," I say, looking ahead at the teacher.

"That too wouldn't help in my case," he responds sheepishly.

The word Case sounds so calming for the first time and even different when he says. I look at him trying to make sense of what he told, but it all goes in vain when he looks right back at me.

"I am not good at Chemistry, but I'll help you out though and most of the time I am involved in my sports practices, so, I think the project would be on your shoulder," he explains, biting his lower lip.

I keep looking at him like a star-struck fan.

"Casey, you are okay with it, right?" he questions, a little confused.

I study his expressions and then my mind reminds me that I need to reply to him.

"Yeah," I reply.

I try to pay attention to Mr Smith and what all things he is mixing inside the test tubes, but with Jason around me, nothing makes sense. Mr Smith is constantly glancing at us so I keep moving the test tubes here and there. I act all cool and pretend to be interested in the class, but the truth is my mind and heart both are focused on Jason. I watch him again from the corner of my eye and realize that he too is looking in my direction. I quickly shook my head down, trying to read the journal, but suddenly I feel him touching my hand. He shifts my hand away from the journal and turns the page over. I look at him a little startled by his touch.

"Casey Dalton, all okay?" I hear Mr Smith.

"Yeah," I say, shifting my gaze to the teacher.

"So, tell me how many minutes the smallest size of a copper sulphate crystal will take to melt?" he questions, pouring water in the test tube.

I am so screwed up. God! I don't want to be thrown out from the class on the very first day.

"If the temperature of water is 70 degrees Celsius, it takes maximum 10 minutes," Jason whispers in my ears.

I exactly repeat what he says and Mr Smith seems happy with my answer.

"Mr Smith, the water is not turning blue." Someone shouts from the other corner and Mr Smith walks to a section which is half visible from ours.

"Thanks," I say, smiling at Jason.

He looks at me and studies me properly. My eyebrows make a little hill on my forehead and before I can ask him something,

"You look prettier when your hair is loose," he says, winking at me.

"Wha ... What?" I say, choking a little.

He smiles back, probably noticing my nervousness and removes the band from my hair. My nervousness multiplies.

"There you go," he says, handing me the rubber band.

I just nod and push away the hair behind my ears. The 'Jason effect' is so powerful that I am not able to move an inch until the class is over. I am so conscious and he on the other hand is himself. Introvert people like me have a tough time dealing with such situations; it's like one in a million years someone as gorgeous as him showers attention on us. I look at him; he strokes away his hair with his milky white fingers. He is like a Greek God and his touch still makes a shiver run through my spine. I instantaneously get goose bumps on my hand. He is like ... like a live electric wire to me.

My heart just keeps skipping beats and it is about to explode, out of happiness because for the first time someone noticed me. He noticed me and my hair and that I look prettier when they are loose. All this while I thought I am invisible to people like him; so gorgeous and so confident who live on the other side of the world; the extroverts.

******

The class gets over and he walks me up to Mr Smith for the project information.

"Estimation of content bone ash and sterilization of water using bleaching powder," Mr Smith reads out the project titles from a list.

"Let me know, if you need any help," Mr Smith adds and leaves the lab.

I quickly note it down while Jason waits for me. I make sure that my handwriting comes out proper and neat. I feel so mediocre when someone so perfect as him stands near me. I keep the book in my bag and at the same time I hear Stella calling out to me.

"Hey," I wave, walking in her direction. The first step in her direction makes me feel so guilty and humiliated about the fact that I didn't bid Jason goodbye. I instantly turn around, but he is nowhere! He just went away, how can he do that?? I feel guiltier now as I was the one who ignored him.

******

"What was he doing here?" Stella questions.

"Do you mean Jason?" I say, confirming.

"Yeah, who else?" she replies, making a deadpan face.

"Oh... Uh ... we are partners in the Chemistry project. So, he was helping me out with the topic," I explain, smiling and walking in the direction of the cafeteria.

"Is that the only reason?" she adds.

"Yeah," I reply.

"Okay," she responds, unconvinced by my answer.

"Why? Do you like him?" I almost giggle.

"No, boys like Jason aren't meant for liking," she replies, typing something in her cell phone.

"What do you mean by that?" I question a little confused.

"He is a player," Stella says curtly.

"Player? Are you kidding me? He was sweet to me the entire time." I say defending him.

She looks at me strangely, studies me for a second and then smiles, no actually laughs!

"What??" I question, a little shocked.

"Miss Casey Dalton likes Jason Ellwood!" She announces.

"No... No," I say, blood rushing to my face.

"Casey, Jason is not a good guy. He will hurt you. Okay?" Stella explains and she seems really serious about all this.

"Okay," I reply, nodding.

"Stay away from him," she adds.

I just nod back like an obedient puppet. I have no idea why Stella's behaviour is so negative towards him. How can he ever hurt anyone? He is so...*BANG* I can't believe what I see. In a fraction of seconds my life changes completely, I feel moisture emerging in my eyes. How can he do this? Why? How can he just ... he just allow her to kiss him?? I choke even in my thoughts.

"I guess, everything is clear now," I hear Stella's voice in my ears.

I look at her and then look at them; Jason and the girl who just kissed him. She almost dived inside him. It is unacceptable to me that someone just kissed Jason, right in front of my eyes. How can he allow her? How? Why?

"Who is she?" I question, sitting beside Stella. By the time I try to accept the unacceptable fact that someone just kissed my Greek God she'd already taken a sandwich. I was hungry too, but a few seconds back, until the guy I have a hopeless crush on gets kissed by someone else.

"She is Lyra Nettleton, his girlfriend," Stella replies, munching her sandwich.

I observe her, she sure deserves him. I am nothing in comparison to her. She is hot! There is no sign of fat on her body, she looks stunning in that short black dress whereas I on the other hand will never be able to wear it, let alone how would I look in that. She seems perfect, adorable eyes, cute nose, lips which are right now moving around Jason's cheek. It disgusts me and so I look away. In the meanwhile Mark, Jessica and Zac arrive. They all are warm towards me and ask me about my day at school.

"Hey Stella," the girl, I mean Lyra, calls out.

"Hey," Stella responds, smiling.

"Got friends with the new girl?" Lyra questions Stella and at the same time looks in my direction. I look at her and notice how she is stuck to Jason.

"Yeah, she is Casey Dalton." Stella introduces me.

She smiles at me and I fake a smile. Jason winks at me and his lips curve into a heart melting smile. The same time Lyra turns towards him and murmurs something in his ear which makes him giggle. It feels terrible to see them together and I pray to God that Stella finishes her sandwich ASAP. I look around and think of Susan. I need to tell her about Jason, she is the only one who will understand me. I quickly remove my phone, but then drop the idea because I can't tell her right now. I can't just walk away and plus I have made friends on the very first day of school, what would they think about me? Another reason behind my decision is Jason. It is like I am glued to the seat and every few seconds I will glance at him. It is like I am on an auto play.

"Casey, do you have any boyfriend or boy best-friend?" Jessica questions.

"Uhh... No. No boyfriend," I reply.

"Do you like anybody at the school?" she adds.

"It's her first day yet, sweetheart," Mark interrupts.

"Not yet," I answer, smiling.

"We have a lot of cute boys in here. I am sure you'll find one for our winter prom at least." Jessica giggles. Yeah there are a whole lot of cute boys here but the one I liked already has a partner.

"How do you find Chicago?" Zac interrupts.

"It's great!" I reply, faking excitement.

"I am sure you won't miss New York," he adds.

"I just miss my best friend," I reply, smiling and thinking about Susan.

"Prom reminds me, Casey ... one of my friends really wants to ask you out, and do you want to meet him?" Stella says, finishing the sandwich.

"I'll let you know," I reply, smiling my best.

All of us bid each other goodbye, including Jason and his girlfriend Lyra. I hold nothing against her, but whenever I see both of them together, I feel something's wrong, terribly wrong. I've had crush on guys who already had a girlfriend or loved someone else, but these two, they just don't fit together or maybe

I am just a little jealous. Stella and I walk to the parking where I'd parked the car earlier this morning.

******

"So, who is he?" I question Stella, as we walk to my car.

"Eric Simpson, he finds you interesting." She says, laughing.

"And when did he see my interestingness?" I too laugh out.

"In the Chemistry lab, when you answered something about copper sulphate," she answers, sitting in the car.

I blush a little because Eric should find Jason interesting instead of me, after all, all my "interestingness" came from him. Technically he helped me out.

"Okay," I reply, pulling the gear.

"So should I tell him that you find him interesting too?" she questions.

"No, not so soon, I am not yet prepared," I say, pretending to be nervous.

I am least interested in Eric, but I can't tell the truth to Stella. She won't like it anyway and bitch more about Jason which I won't be able to handle.

"He likes you anyway, don't be so nervous," she assures.

I just nod and before we can discuss more on that her phone rings.

"Yeah, I am so sorry sweetheart. I am reaching in 5," she mumbles in a baby voice.

She disconnects the call and tells me to stop the car. She hugs me and tells me that she is sorry because she forgot to tell me about her boyfriend and also that she'll tell me everything tomorrow. I assure her that it is okay and not to make a big deal out of it. She gets out of the car and I drive myself home.

******

On the way home the only person I think of is Jason. I play and replay our entire conversation, but yet can't find the reason behind Stella's behaviour towards him. Well, I know he is a flirt, but who isn't?? Maybe, just maybe, I misinterpreted his actions. The rosy picture of him and his girlfriend occupies my mind and I realize that he is different with her. He is happy but not really, the twinkle in his eyes is missing or maybe I am finding out reasons to make myself happy because I can't accept them together. Particularly, there isn't anything about him that is driving me crazy. I mean, I have seen guys, guys who are better than him but he, he affects me badly.

There is something in his smile, the way his eyes twinkle, those I-am-at-peace eyes, the way he strokes away his hair; his golden-ish black hair, his hands, his touch, his voice; it's so mysterious and velvety at the same time, the way he bites his lower lip. I wonder what it would be to kiss them, will they melt in mine or will mine melt in them; I'd prefer the latter. I can almost hear my heartbeats now. This is what he does, he makes me nervous and the same time makes me want that nervousness. I blink my eyes and the image of Lyra and Jason kissing each other flashes in front of me. I take a deep breath and pull the car into the parking. Quickly, I remove the keys and open the door. Keeping my bag aside on the couch I walk to the kitchen dialling Susan's number.

"Hey, I was about to call you," she says, receiving it.

"Umm... Susan," I choke a little, framing the sentence in my mind.

"What? Do you like someone?? Tell me, who is he? Is he cute? Or hot...?" she keeps questioning me and I don't know how, she guesses every time what's going in my mind.

"No," I lie, killing her excitement.

"Okay," she replies, her voice fading away.

"Susan, how do you always figure out what's going on in my mind?" I question her.

"What?" she asks and I feel the confusion in her voice.

"You like someone, don't you?" she shouts in excitement.

"Yes," I reply.

"Tell me everything, now!" she screams out like a little child.

"His name is Jason, we met in the Chemistry lab and he is well, HOT," I tell her, pursing my lips.

"Aw, so did you guys talk?" she questions.

"Yeah, we had a small conversation and most of the time he was trying to flirt, can you imagine that? He noticed me. Who notices people like me?" I question blushing.

"Excuse me, what do you mean by 'people like me'? You don't know Casey, but you are beautiful. Stop underestimating yourself." She shouts a little and this time I sense the seriousness in her voice, but just because she changes her tone it doesn't mean I'll believe her.

"Really...?" I question

"Of course! Why will I lie?" she argues.

"Okay," I end the topic.

"Wait, you don't believe me, right?" she says.

"I believe you," I reply.

"Great, now continue the story." she orders.

"So, we had a little talk and he is my partner in the Chemistry project, but the sad part is he has a very, very hot girlfriend and I stand no chance in front of her. Also, I think he doesn't like me that way," I explain to her, walking back to the couch.

"You are hot too, so what if he has a girlfriend?" Susan says curtly.

"Susan, he has a girlfriend and I am not a boyfriend stealer!" I reply

"Fine!" Susan says and hangs up.

I call her again, but she seems too generous in not receiving the call. I sit on the couch; with arms around my legs and rest my head on the knees. I glance at the time; Dad will be home anytime now. The moment these 3 letters – DAD – come to my mind I is struggling again. So, do I tell him about Jason or do I not? I keep thinking about this for another 5 minutes and prefer the latter. I will tell him sometime soon, but not today because I myself seem startled and confused regarding my feelings about Jason. I walk to the bathroom and look at myself. A moment later, I realize that I indeed look pretty when my hair is loose. I have long black messy hair and they end just near my waist line, which are also the only best thing about me.

"Still, I stand no chance against Lyra." I murmur, analyzing my body.

I walk to the kitchen and start preparing dinner, but in the back of my mind I am still stuck on Jason. Did he actually love Lyra? Does he? If he does, then why would he flirt with me? Why will a guy like him even notice me, let alone the part about my hair. Why? I have no answers to all these unanswerable questions. Maybe everyone is a flirt; maybe he just did all that for fun, maybe. Gosh! Look what he is making me do? I am constantly thinking about him, this is so not done.

"Casey Dalton, just accept the things as they are." I order myself.

I take a deep breath and murmur, "I can't."

The questions start popping in my head like pop up ads. Suddenly, Stella's words echo in my mind. "He is a player." Why would she say that? At first, I think maybe she too likes him, but she already has a boyfriend, so it isn't making any sense. This is all too much to handle for my fragile heart.

Chapter 3

The dinner is almost done; roasted vegetable chicken and chocolate milkshake. My mind is a terrible mess and so I decide to chill out for a little while. I run the water tap on, pour some bubble soap and let the bath tub fill up. I play some music and then allow myself to rest in the bath tub. The water dancing with the rhythm of music all over my body and the smell of my strawberry bubble soap fills my nostrils. Within seconds, I find myself smiling and humming the same song. I allowed the water to dance for a little while and then I am out when I hear Dad knocking the door. I quickly dress up and walk to the living room.

"Honey, you smell of strawberries a little too much," my dad murmurs, planting a small kiss on my forehead.

"How was school?" he adds, sitting on the couch.

"Good. The school is nice, I made a couple friends," I inform him, walking to the kitchen.

"Case, honey, I need to tell you something," I hear him say.

"Yeah, Dad... I am listening," I respond, removing the dishes.

"Would you come here for a second, honey ... it's important," he says a little louder.

I walk to the couch and snuggle beside him. The water dripping down my hair sends goose bumps all over my body. I cuddle a little into the couch and wait for my Dad to speak something.

"Honey, don't over react on this, okay?" he says and waits for my answer. I nod with an assuring smile.

"Jennifer proposed to me..." Before he can complete I interrupt in between.

"What? When...?" I ask almost surprised.

"Today, like an hour ago or maybe..." he replies, looking at the clock.

"So, what did you say??" I almost shout a little excited.

He is quiet and purses his lips. A moment later, I understand his silence.

"I am okay with it Dad, like completely. I do like her a lot. You should go for it," I explain to him, smiling all the while, but deep inside my heart I am a little uncomfortable. Also, I know somewhere that this will be coming one day and for me all I want is my Dad to be happy, always. On the other hand Jen (Jennifer) is a wonderful person. We've met several times and each time she was warm towards me. Well, once she even tried hooking me up with a guy so, I think I am completely okay with my Dad getting married to her.

"Are you sure, Case?" he questions looking straight into my eyes.

"Yes Daddy, I am sure," I assure him, looking back into his eyes.

"So did she call?" I ask out the details.

"No, she got herself a transfer too and is here in Chicago! Can you believe that?" he says, his eyes popping out.

"Wow! That's really sweet of her and I think we have made her wait for quite a while now," I reply.

"So, should I call her right now? Or you know ... like..." It is so adorable to see Dad all confused and also the fact that he waited for my answer first. I mean, he could have just accepted the proposal and later on explained everything to me but he didn't. So, if he being a father can do so much, I being his daughter need to make this moment special in his life. After all you live only once and Jen, on the other hand, isn't an evil step mother.

I tell Dad to take her out for dinner and to counter propose to her. I also tell him to take her favourite flowers and the most important thing, 'the ring', which will bind them together. Dad leaves after some twenty minutes, which probably went in deciding what he should wear and asking me a zillion times whether he looks good and etcetera. Well, to be precise he is nervous.

"And Dad, now you may kiss the bride," I say winking at him.

He smiles and plants a peck on my forehead. I watch him drive away from the gate. I take a deep breath and walk to the kitchen, smiling and thinking about the food I've cooked. I quickly drink some milk and keep all the food in the refrigerator. I am happy that Dad finally has someone who makes him complete. I think about the both of them for a little while and then decide to visit the church that is nearby; also I need to explore Chicago! (Kidding). I get my coat, lock the house properly and walk to the church I'd seen a few blocks away on the way to school. Thousands of things keep running in my mind. I knew one day all this would be happening, like Dad would marry Jen, but maybe I am not prepared yet. Today is particularly a messy day, how could have I not known about it? I burned my favourite blouse, then met Jason who later turned to be a complete different person than what I'd imagined, Stella's warning, also Susan's arguments and last, but not the least Jen proposing to Dad, although that is a good news, but the thought that now I need to share my second best friend with someone else makes me uncomfortable. Today; precisely isn't my day!

******

The air is colder than usual and anytime the snow may hit the ground. It is a foggy night and there is no one near the church side. But walking back seems to be a waste, so I quickly walk inside the church, my footsteps echoing all around. I take a candle and light it up with the help of another, placing it into the candle holder. The church is empty and I feel a little awkward and scared so I decide to leave as soon as I finish my short prayer. I sit in the first row and murmur the prayer.

"Amen," I say and smile. I immediately turn around and start walking to the gate. As soon as I am out of the church I glance around, it is a little darker and it be better if I rush back home quickly. As I turn around to walk I see two shadows forming ahead of me in the dimly lit light of the side walk. There are two middle heighted males, not far behind from me. I quickly take a step ahead and hear, a drunken voice,

"Woo...hoo, man look at her, she is hot."

I so want to punch that bastard in his face, but instead I walk a step ahead and I sense someone right behind me. I close my eyes shut, my heartbeats racing and I keep cursing myself and that if I reach home safely I am never going to linger around alone in Chicago. I try to move, but my body isn't listening any of it. I can't move and nor do I have the courage to turn back when,

"You smell of strawberries..." I hear a familiar voice, I swallow the saliva down my throat and turn around, it is him; Jason. I sigh in relief and turn around. The guy who shouted out is over the phone with someone and I can't get much of what he is saying as all I hear are the words, "I'll kill you", "Fuck you", "You are a whore". It is clear that his heart is broken by the one he is talking to.

It takes me no time to realize that Jason is right beside me, inches away. I look at him and he looks a little weirder, but in a cute way. He seems drunk too. He looks at me the way a kid looks at a chocolate bar; I mean it's so adorable. I take a glance at him; he is wearing a rough pair of jeans, a white T-shirt and a black leather jacket. Well, he does stink a little, but the strawberry bubble soap covers it.

"What are you doing here?" he mumbles, and I look at his lips and then his eyes. He isn't even blinking that much.

"I came to the church." I reply blushing.

Although, we are inches away from each other I literally feel the warmth of his body. He smiles like a little child. I hate people who drink, but when it comes to him, I didn't know someone looks so beautiful when drunk, I know boys aren't meant to be beautiful, but he is and hot too.

"Are you drunk?" I question him.

"No, not at all," he says.

I laugh it out loud and a little disappointment emerges in his eyes.

"I am not drunk," he says a little firmly now, but the firmness of his voice works nowhere when I see his face. His face has that childish expression, the one we had when we were kids and tried to explain to our parents that the tooth fairy was for real and they just wouldn't believe and then we would fake an angry expression, yeah, the same. So, he is indeed drunk.

"Okay, I got it," I say trying hard not to laugh.

He looks at his bottle and puts it near his mouth. Before I take it from him, we both realize that it is already empty. A second later, the bottle lands on the road all broken. Jason has just thrown it out of anger which isn't really anger.

"Bad manners," I remark and I shift a little away from the broken pieces.

"Aw, sorry," he says, immediately making a puppy face and comes closer.

"That's okay," I say looking in his dark emerald eyes. I also didn't know people when drunk can be so awesome. I like the drunk-Jason more and now that I like him this way it is impossible for me to look away from his eyes, let alone go home.

"Where do you live?" I question him, thinking I'll at least walk him home; his home.

He doesn't answer, but instead puts his hand in his jacket. I pray he doesn't remove another bottle of beer out from it. The same time my cell phone beeps, it is a text message from Dad:

"Hon, I am staying at Jen's...she is really happy and wants to meet you. Thank you for being such a wonderful daughter, I'll see you in the morning. Sweet Dreams Love you."

So, the day which didn't seem "my day", somehow gets converted into "my day." I look at Jason, his hand is still underneath his jacket and he is desperately searching for something. So, before my phone buzzes loudly and spoils everything I quickly type a text back:

"And thank you for always being such a wonderful father, love you more."

I roll my eyes on Jason, he is looking back at me, and God knows how long he's been looking that way. I notice a red rose in his hand and I wonder what the "drunk-Jason" would want to do now. I feel him going completely out of hand and all I want is to get him home safely. I look for his friend and he has completely disappeared. He is gone.

"Jason, where's your friend?" I question him, panicking.

"What friend...?" he questions, looking at the rose.

"The one who came with you, both of you were drunk? Remember?" I say, trying to help him recall his friend.

"I am not drunk!" He shouts a little.

"Okay," I reply, busy thinking what to do now. Both of us can't stand the entire night here. It is risky.

"Jason, do you mind telling me your address??" I question.

He doesn't answer and comes an inch closer, lifting his hand to show the rose.

"For you, my lady, the love of my life," he mumbles and I can't stop laughing. I mean what is he doing?? It is cute, but still I will prefer all this if he will be in his senses.

He touches his index finger to my lips and his touch makes me shiver a little. He inches himself more close and now our bodies almost touch each other. I try breaking the eye contact but it is impossible. He inches his face closer and his lips now are so close to mine that I can feel his breath on my face. He shifts his finger aside and cups my face with one hand, dragging me closer by the waist using another. He parts his lips and touches mine. His lips don't taste bitter, they are sweet. He grabs me a little more close to himself and kisses me more firmly. My lips melting on his, eyes closed, my hands reach for his neck, our bodies touching each other, now. I am losing my breath, but Jason wants more of me. His eyes are still close, his lips slowly parting away, still kissing mine before he finally lets them go. He opens his eyes and meets my gaze. He plants a kiss on my forehead, right after that and pulls me into his embrace. I feel his breath around my ear.

"You are sweet," he murmurs and kisses my hair. His icy cold lips touch my ear and I cuddle into him out of cold.

My head resting on his chest I suddenly realize that he is drunk and that this is wrong. I slowly part him away from myself, not that I want to, but I am helpless.

"Jason lets walk you home," I tell him.

He doesn't say anything but pulls me closer to himself and hugs me back, this time more tightly.

"It's not safe, it's too late, and we need to get you home," I say in his ears.

******

He doesn't answer any of my questions and before he dozes off here, on the road, I need to get him home. It is too late to call anyone and ask for his address and neither does his friend seem anywhere. So, I decide to take him home, my home. While walking back home, he still holds me close enough. I don't feel like asking him anything because I know he is in his own fantasy world right now, let alone he would listen to me. In a matter of minutes we reach home and I open the door.

"Sit here and don't move, okay?" I tell him, making him sit on the couch.

I walk to the kitchen to bring some milk for him, but when I come back he is already asleep. I am too lazy to walk back to the kitchen so I myself drink the milk. Later, I walk to my room and grab two blankets, a note book and a pen. I come to him and cover him with the blanket, he looks angelic. God knows what he's dreaming about; I kiss him on his forehead and start writing a note:

Wake me up before you leave or need something, I am leaving the pain killer on the table in case you get a hangover!

I place the note on the table near the couch, there it will be visible to him clearly and then remove the painkiller, leaving it on the dining table. Later, I set the alarm just in case I am not able to wake up before Dad arrives. He would take this the other way around and also tell Jen to ask me whether I am virgin or not! I recline on the couch and watch him sleep. So, I did really kiss him. It was probably the best moment of my life. I keep recalling the entire kiss in my mind about ten thousand times. On the other hand, I realize how wrong it is. The best and the moment which seems so right and perfect can also be wrong if I look from the other side. I can't even blame him, he was drunk but I wasn't. I could have stopped him, but that very moment I just couldn't. I was so enchanted by him. No one is immune to such situations and also when someone as gorgeous as Jason would be right there, his lips so close to mine. I am feeling different and guilty, both at the same time. Then another thought pops in my head, will he even remember kissing me? Will he? If he remembers will he ever talk to me? What if he just breaks whatever he has with me? And what if Lyra finds out all this? Gosh, these questions are never ending. The night is sleepless, first because he is right there, there in front of me. Although he is sleeping, but still he has me captivated the way he looks right now. And second, because I have no idea about the circumstances a pure thing as kiss, could create. I keep looking at him, still replaying the entire conversation that we had and the best moment of my life. Jason, on the other hand is sleeping a sound sleep, he doesn't even move a little and for a second I focus on his breathing to make sure he is alive. He is so damn still like, like a real Greek God or to be precise drunken Greek God. I never want this night to end, never or if we both wake up in an altogether different world away from all this then it is okay, then I will be okay if the night ends. On the other hand, if going to church brings a Greek God into my life then I think I'll go on a regular basis and pray that every day I find my drunk-Jason.

Now I know what love feels like.

******

I have no idea when I slept, the last time I checked the time it was 4:35 in the morning, but the alarm woke me up. My eyes are too heavy and I am not in any mood of opening them either. Then like a pop up ad, my mind makes me remember about Jason. I am up immediately, no not with the fear of Dad, but I want to wake him up. I look around and I don't see him.

"Jason...?" I call out to him, walking around.

He is nowhere, I walk back to the couch and see the note, and it looks a little longer. Jason has written something for me:

Wake me up before you leave or need something, I am leaving the pain killer on the table in case you get a hangover!

I am so sorry about last night, thanks for the pain killer. I didn't feel like waking you up.

P.S. you look really cute, when you're asleep.

I smile like a little child after reading his note. I look away and see that he's left the rose, the one he is giving me last night. I am super sleepy, but it is important to hide the note and the rose so, I take both the blankets and climb upstairs to my room. I keep the note and the rose in the closet and then jump on the bed. I use Jason's blanket instead of mine and it smells of him in a way. I inhale his smell and fall asleep, right away. I am awakened with the loud knocks at the door and someone shouting my name.

"Case, you okay?" I hear Dad shout, as I open the door.

"Yeah, why...?" I question shaking my head a little.

"What why? I have been knocking your door from past fifteen minutes!" he shouts again.

"Dad," I say.

"What?" he says still shouting.

"Stop shouting, I am fine. Really, See..." I assure him, turning around and throwing my hands halfway in the air.

"Everything fine in here?" Jen questions.

"Yeah, it's just my Dad ... uhh ... you know he loves me a lot," I explain, winking.

"That he sure does," she replies, hugging me and kisses me on my cheeks.

"Both of you, I am making the breakfast, go get freshen up," she orders and walks out of the room.

"Wow, she really seems to take this Mom thing seriously," I say joking.

Dad joins me and then I ask him to give me all the details about last night (except what happened at Jen's place). He starts telling me everything, that he was late and Jen was already there waiting for him and he felt so embarrassed for a while. When asked the reason behind him being late, he was all confused buying the flowers and it took him about fifteen minutes to decide which one would be the best and ended up with red roses. Roses make me remember the rose that Jason had given me. Later, he was so nervous that he couldn't even eat properly and like a baby dropped the soup here and there. Jen couldn't stop laughing all this while. After dinner things were pretty normal, my Dad proposed to her and she agreed to be the bride. After narrating me the whole incident, he goes downstairs to help Jen. I open the closet and read and reread the note several times. I am about to kiss the rose when I hear Dad shout again,

"Case...Honey... Come down."

I kiss the rose and rush downstairs. Jen has prepared pancakes and scrambled eggs.

"When are you getting married?" I ask my mouth full with scrambled eggs.

"What?" both of them explode together.

I almost choke for a second and then ask, "Yeah, like officially?"

"Soon," Jen says and Dad nods with her answer. It is so much fun to make them nervous.

"Case, did you sleep on the couch last night?" he questions.

Okay, so now the bottle of nervousness points me. "Na, No, I was just watching a movie..." I lie.

"Okay," he says.

The rest of the time we discuss things except marriage and soon both of them leave for their respective jobs. The day seems normal, just that I get two pecks on the forehead today. The second I am alone all the memories of last night flash back.

******

I walk to my room, run the tap for the bath tub to fill and today for a change I use peach and orchid bubble soap. Bathing is okay, but the problem which makes my room a mess is what do I wear? In around five minutes my room is upside down. I still haven't figured out what would he like on me. So, with my not-so-hot wardrobe I have limited choices. I can either wear a skirt or a dress. The problem with skirt is I am not able to find the blouse which suits it. It is later I realize that I'd burnt it yesterday with my own hands. Somewhere in my mind I am cursing Samantha. The one who'd screwed up my blouse. So now the only option remains is the dress. Before getting dressed up I once again check the schedule and the word 'Chemistry' makes me blush and hasten my heartbeats. I analyze the dress minutely because it's been a while since I've put it on; it isn't torn or damaged from anywhere, thank God! The dress isn't too much of a big deal but Susan always likes me in this particular dress. Susan reminds me, I still haven't inform her about last night and right now if I call her I'll be late for school, let alone the time I need to get ready.

I decide to call her after school or maybe late night. I get the dress over my body and it fits well. The dress highlights my body line perfectly, it's a plain causal sleeveless dress in peach colour and has a criss cross back, ending above my knees. Now the part remains were my hair. But today I want to try something different; well to be precise I want to look different. I search among all the drawers for the hairclip that Susan gifted me last year. Finally, after fidgeting for about 2 minutes and 33 seconds, victory is mine. I brush my hairs to the left side, gathering them to make a side-ponytail. Once the hair is secured I use a rubber band to tie them up. Later, I remove some strands of hair out, securing half of them with the heart shaped clip, making a little puff. The ponytail comes perfect, with some strands of hair around my face. I search for the lip gloss and apply it on my lips, making them shine a little. I spray the right amount of perfume not that I need it, the bubble soap is enough and I don't want much of attention in the Chemistry lab. I accompany my dress with ballet shoes as I am not comfortable wearing heels. I look *decently* hot; well that's what Susan says. There is a lot of Susan happening in my mind, since morning so, I finally text her:

Morning, I am really sorry about last time... call you ASAP. Miss you.

I miss Susan today, I mean right now if she'd be here, I wouldn't be so nervous and also that my room wouldn't be such a mess. I take a final glance at myself, pack my bag, lock the house properly and then I am off to meet my Greek God.

Chapter 4

I head towards my car, I hear a robin chirping. I look over the tree and it flies away, immediately. I smile at it and sit inside the car, driving it all the way to Stella's house. I stop the car right in front of her house and press the horn twice. She comes rushing through the door, with an apple in her hand and gets into the car.

"Someone's looking beautiful," she remarks, admiring me from top to toe.

I shoot a look at her which clearly means I don't believe her.

"What...?" she says, biting the apple.

I laugh it off and in a corner of my mind I am fighting over and over whether to tell her about last night or not, I decide that I will first meet Jason and then tell her everything.

"Stella...?" I say, pulling the gear.

"Yeah...?" she replies.

"I think you promised me something yesterday," I say, looking at her.

She rolls her eyes, and then smiles, "Yeah, I remember I have to tell you about my boyfriend," she adds.

"His name is Kevin Mathew, we met at a social gathering and then hit it off together," she says.

"He is not in our school?" I question

"No, he works with his Dad. He is five years elder to me," she says, searching something in her cell phone. A second later, she shows me a picture. Both look great together, like a perfect couple. Somewhere my heart is lost in day dreams again.

"You both look great together," I tell her, smiling.

As she finishes her apple, she talks more about Kevin, and we reach school. I park the car and we head for our classes.

"I like you hair clip," she remarks, still observing me.

"Thanks and stop looking at me like that." I order her.

She blinks her eyes and adds, "You seem prepared."

"Prepared for what?" I ask

"To meet him..." she says, throwing her hands in the air.

I nod and smile back. While walking I notice Lyra, she is alone. I look all around, but Jason is nowhere. Well, I want to talk to her, but this isn't the right time. The only person I need now is Jason. Stella and I have the same classes back to back until break followed by Algebra, Biology and Literature. The Algebra class gets over in a jiffy, because the entire time we were focused on solving sums. I got three out of five correct; the remaining two sums were tricky and I had to wrack my brain. Stella helped me with them and when the class was over I'd all of them done. Biology is extremely boring; with Mr Mathews' extremely slow moving PPT presentation. I mentally start counting seconds in my mind when,

"Don't you have a boyfriend?" Stella whispers.

"No," I reply, nodding my head sideways. The word 'boyfriend' diverts my entire attention towards Jason.

"Never...?" she whispers, again.

"Never." I reply, smiling awkwardly.

"Are you kidding me?" she says a little shocked.

"Well, do I really sound like that?" I ask.

"Don't you tell me that, Casey Dalton you never dated a guy?" she exclaims.

"Nope..." I mutter through my teeth.

"You never ever liked anyone in your entire life?" she says over reacting.

"What entire life, I am still seventeen," I correct her.

"Well, I did like someone in my third grade, but he turned out to be a real dumbass," I add.

"Third grade...?" she questions.

"Yeah," I say.

"No I mean that's it...? You never liked anyone else after that?" she explodes.

I smile awkwardly.

"Aw, that's awful," she says.

"I dated three guys before finally devoting my heart and soul to Kevin," she confesses.

I just smile back because I have no idea how to react to it. Awkward silence follows us; I never plan to date someone or like someone. I feel if something's meant to happen it will happen. I am not saying that I am a princess waiting for my prince, NO! All I mean is, if someone is going to be a part of my life, a part of me, it will happen and I wouldn't even realize it. It will happen, down a few days, a few years but it will and I am in no hurry.

"I am sure, you'll find someone soon," she says, breaking the silence.

"Yeah, I hope so," I reply.

"By the way, he just texted me that, you look really pretty today," she adds.

"What?" I say shocked. Why will Jason text her? Forget about him texting her, the thing is how can she be so okay with it. I mean, by now she would have warned me a million times to stay away from him. I immediately sense that something is definitely wrong.

"Eric, just texted me see..." she adds, showing me the message which says; *I can't get my eyes off Casey.* Wait a second, WHAT THE HELL IS GOING ON?

"Eric...?" I ask, confused.

"The one for whom you have come all dressed up," she answers.

"Wait. What?" I question, totally confused.

"The guy we were talking about yesterday, in the car...?" she replies, trying to remind me.

"Yeah, I remember, Eric, right," I say assuring her.

Gosh! Stella thinks I am all dressed up to meet Eric. All this while, she was thinking that I was talking about Eric and not Jason. SHIT! This is gonna be a real confusion now. While Bio created all the confusion, Literature seems like never ending. The class is so boring that I am again forced to mentally count seconds in my mind, Stella is completing her notes and so I think not to disturb her. I am about to bump myself into Jason's thoughts and just then I hear Stella's voice.

"Kevin gifted me this yesterday," she informs showing me a chain. The chain has a heart shaped pendant which opens into two parts, the left side had their picture and on the right side were the words, "*till death do us apart.*"

"This is really beautiful," I say. I am already feeling guilty about the fact that I am not able to tell her about Jason.

She blushes like a small child. "We completed a year of being together, yesterday," she informs, still smiling.

"Wow, that's really great," I say and then I remember, I can at least tell her about my Dad's marriage.

"Stella," I say.

"Yeah..?" she replies.

"My Dad is gonna get married," I inform her.

"Really, who is she?" she asks.

"Jennifer, she is really sweet," I answer.

"When did all this happen?" she questions.

"Yesterday, Jennifer proposed to my Dad but he waited to discuss the thing with me," I explain.

"So, what did you tell him?" she asks anxiously.

"I told him that I was okay and also I made him propose to her," I say, winking.

"Quite a day it was," I add, remembering everything.

"I am so excited," she says and the same time the class gets over.

We walk to the cafeteria looking for everyone, to be precise Jason. Stella needs a book from her locker. Locker reminds me, I still haven't been allotted a locker and I need to ask the office staff for the same. The locker room is on the way to the cafeteria so I accompany her. The room is large enough, almost the size of a classroom. It has rows of lockers all around, similar to a library. Stella is busy finding her stuff so I think to look around a little. Two rows ahead, I hear some whispers,

"I love you so much," I hear a female voice and then the voices disappear.

I walk a step forward and peep ahead to find out what is going on. There are two of them, standing in a corner opposite to mine. I can't see the faces at first, the guy is leaning against the locker and the girl is all over him, a moment later their lips are engrossed into each other. The girl, she is almost falling all over the guy and her hands...

"Casey, its bad manners," Stella suddenly whispers in my ears and scares the shit out of me.

"Oh ... uh ... I am just trying to find out who they are, I mean locker room isn't an appropriate place for making out," I whisper back. Stella laughs out, once we are out of the locker room.

"Lyra has an all time hormonal problem," Stella adds.

"Woah, is she cheating around?" I question I don't know what happens to me when Stella speaks of Lyra or Jason, I just can't help to dig more information on any of them.

"No way, it was Jason. I don't think she'd cheat on Jason inside the school," she answers, guessing.

Before I can spy more on them, Mark, Jessica and Zac greet us. I smile and greet them back, but inside I am ripping apart. The images of Jason and Lyra, from the locker room, keep flashing in front of my eyes. Why did he do this to me? I can't breathe; every breath I take the broken pieces of my heart ache. My lungs demand air, but the more I inhale the more it pains. I just want to run somewhere and cry until I am immune to this heart ache.

"The new girl seems lost," I hear someone speaking.

******

It is hard to come back from the world where I am right now; it is dark in here; dark enough where no one would be able see the scars, the bruises on my heart. A place, where the demons keep haunting our souls; each time our damage souls fight back, but only becoming one of them in the end. And here, I may leave my broken heart, either it fights back and heals or it loses and becomes one of them.

"Casey, Case..." I hear someone shout.

"Yea...h..." I murmur and open my eyes. I'd passed out and I don't exactly remember when, but I hate my new school, and Lyra and Jason and Chicago and the whole darn world!

"I am fine," I say, sitting upright.

"You okay?" Stella questions, warily.

I just nod and sip a little orange juice.

"I am good, just ... there's nothing to worry," I assure everyone. Mark, Jessica and Zac too seem a little worried.

"Should I call your Dad? Or maybe drive you home?" Stella adds.

"No. I am Fine." I say it more like an order. I eat a burger because passing out in the Chemistry lab doesn't captivate me enough. Plus I have to get answers from that moron Jason Ellwood. Stella walks me to the chemistry lab; Mr Smith hasn't showed up yet.

"You want me to switch the class with you?" she questions for the fifth time now.

"Stella, I am Fine." I mutter through my teeth.

"Okay fine, but in case you feel dizzy or something, call me or your father or someone who would drive you home," she shouts a little and leaves for her class.

I walk inside the lab; everyone is probably on their respective sections and waiting for Mr Smith to show up. I quietly walk towards my section, my eyes on the floor. I sense too many eyeballs on me and become a little conscious. I settle and in a blink of an eye, he is standing right beside me, wearing a light blue worn out jeans and a black T-shirt.

"You okay?" he questions immediately.

I look into in his eyes, thinking what makes him ask that question.

"Let me break your heart and ask you, are you okay?" I want to tell him on his face, but instead I just give a half smile. God knows why on earth, he's even bothered to ask me that.

"Heard you passed out in the cafeteria," he adds.

"Yeah, I did," I reply.

"You look different today, like ... kind of ... gorgeous," he says, observing me.

I so want to punch him in his face. How can he just do this to me? Is it a game? I fake a smile and take a deep breath. This is getting all over me now; it's either me or Lyra. He can't just play around whenever he feels so.

"Hey... why did you kiss me last night?" I question, looking into his eyes.

"Uhh... Kiss...?" he questions back a little shocked.

"Yes, last night, near the church...?" I add.

"Casey, I don't remember anything about last night. I only remember waking up at your house. So, you need to tell me everything," he explains, rolling his eyes.

Wait. What? He doesn't remember anything? He doesn't remember kissing me?? He doesn't remember anything about last night?? Now that really does hurt me. It hurts me more than watching him and Lyra kiss each other. It is unbelievable.

"What do you mean you don't remember??" I shout a little looking around.

"Casey Dalton, all okay?" The girl from the nearby section asks. The nearby section seems to be interested in our conversation more than required.

"Yeah, all okay," I say.

"So, you mean to say, you just kissed me like that??" I whisper. I still don't believe he doesn't remember kissing me.

"No, maybe because I think you're totally kissable," he whispers back smiling.

"Wha...?" Before I say something, he interrupts.

"Look, I am not joking around, I seriously don't remember anything." He sighs.

So, he isn't joking. He.IS.SERIOUS. The dagger in my heart pierces a little deeper. I am silent, I have nothing to say, there is nothing left to say. The only thing that goes in my mind is; he doesn't remember kissing me. I don't think the kiss we shared is forgettable, at least not for me.

"Did I really kiss you?" he questions, a little tensed, coming closer.

"No," I lie, looking at a test tube. I look around the lab, but yet there isn't any sign of Mr Smith.

"You smell sweet," he murmurs and for a second it seems like it isn't him, but the drunk-Jason, who'd kissed me last night.

"Jason, are you sure you don't remember anything?" I ask out of suspicion.

"What do you think?" he says, winking.

The same time Stella's sharp words echo my ears, "He is a player." What does he think of himself? Playing with somebody's feelings isn't a cool thing. My mind is collapsing distinguishing between the truth and the lie. He is not what I think he is.

"Casey," he calls out.

"Yeah...?" I say coming out of thoughts, still confused.

"I don't remember kissing you last night, but I do remember kissing you while you were asleep on the couch," he says and I feel his voice getting mischievous. I regretted sleeping that very moment.

"What?? Jason you are such..." I am about to complete, but he interrupts.

"Whoa, chill out. It was just a peck, that too on your forehead, a return gift for the painkiller," he explains, winking again.

I smile back, but now I doubt everything he says. I so want to switch the time backwards and change everything.

"Did you get the note?" he questions, typing something in his phone.

I want to snatch that phone and hit him with that on his head, maybe then he would remember everything or just confess that he is pretending to forget. I don't reply I don't feel the need to. I stare down the window into the trees.

"Case, did you get the note?" I hear his voice; this time more determined. I almost feel his breath on my ear. A shiver trails down my spine.

I turn around and say, "Yes."

"And the rose...?" he adds.

I nod back in reply. Why is he sprinkling salt on my wounded heart, it aches more, but the pain is bearable.

"Why did you leave the red rose for me?" I question, anger rising in my heart.

"Because, people like you are hard to find," he says.

"What do you mean by people like me?" I add. Wow, he knows I would believe him easily. People like me are fools.

"What I mean is that you are really sweet and different," he tries to explain.

In the back of my mind it goes, why don't you just tell me the truth, that'll be better. Say it C'mon. Tell me I am a fool.

"Casey, you are different, I mean who would take a drunken stranger home and take care of him the way you did?" he adds.

What does he mean? Is he playing around again?

"Anyone would," I reply, coming out of the thoughts.

"I don't think so," he says defending.

"Why? Wouldn't you take me home, if you find me drunk on a deserted road?" I ask him. I want to know what he replies. Will he too do the same for me? Will he? Or he will just leave me on my own?

"Uhh... yes I would, but look, what I am talking here is about how much you know me. Taking a drunken monster that you hardly know, to your house, when you are all alone, needs courage," he says.

Okay, now what is he up to? Why is he trying to be so nice? I am so totally confused when it comes to him, how can he just do that? How? It's like every time I meet him, he comes out to be someone else.

"I don't think you fit the title of monster," I say, smiling and to lighten the situation.

"Then...?" he questions.

"I'd rather call you a 'misguided drunken angel'," I say.

"Well, in that case, Ms Casey Dalton what do I call you?" he questions.

"Huh...?" I say.

"If someone as beautiful as you would title me as an angel, though a little misguided and drunken puts me into extreme dilemma, as I wouldn't know what title would describe you and your beauty," he explains.

I just keep smiling. HE THINKS I AM BEAUTIFUL!

"I'd title you as; 'My alluring Knight in the shining Armour'," he says, like a drama queen.

"I think that'd be too much," I say, laughing a little.

"No, I think it's perfect. I am the 'misguided drunken angel' and you, 'my alluring knight', who always saves me from danger," he says, smiling.

I smile back, more like blushing. The only word, that sticks my mind is "MY", I am 'his' alluring knight. Does he really mean that? Or it's just a title?

"Mr Smith won't be taking the class today and the last class is cancelled due to an important meeting." There is an announcement in the class, which brings me back to life.

"Hungry?" Jason questions me.

"Not much," I reply.

"Well, I am," he says and the same time my cell phone beeps. It is Stella; *the last class is cancelled don't leave without me P.S. the class is too boring.*

We walk to the cafeteria and Jason grabs a burger, French fries and coke. I grab a cheese sandwich and look around.

"Where is Lyra?" I question.

"What are you doing Casey? Why are you talking to him? You should stay away from Jason." I tell myself, but no use. He has hypnotized me already!

"I don't know," he replies, munching the burger. He seems lost in the food as of now and so I focus on mine. I've almost finished my sandwich when my cell phone beeps. It is Susan; *call me ASAP.* I quickly reply back, *okay, right now in chem lab.* I have to lie because if by any chance I'll mention Jason's name in the message, my phone would have been flooded with messages and phone calls.

"Boyfriend...?" Jason questions me and I notice that he's finished a burger, fries and coke within 5 minutes.

"No," I reply, keeping the phone on the table.

"You don't have or he didn..." Before he completes, I interrupt.

"No, I don't have a boyfriend."

"Lyra, is your girlfriend, right?" I ask. I don't know what makes me ask that question it is so obvious.

He laughs out and then replies, "Yeah, unfortunately."

"What?" I add.

But before I know the reason behind his laughter, everyone arrives. Lyra, Zac, Jessica, Mark and Stella; she shoots me an angry look. I know the reason behind it. Jason bids me bye and goes away with Lyra; this moment is the most disappointing one.

"Feeling good now?" Zac questions sitting beside me.

"Yeah, much better," I reply.

I do not feel like talking to anyone. It is killing me from inside, I wish I can run away somewhere but I just can't. I am glued to that chair, I can't move an inch. The thoughts torture me, haunt me. Suddenly, I hear my cell phone beep. I expect it to be Susan, but it is Stella; *Eric is waiting outside, follow me when I leave and do not speak about it to Jessica.* A moment later, Stella gets up and walks outside. I remember I have to follow her so after a few seconds I follow her out. She is standing near a car; Eric probably is leaning on it.

"What the hell is happening in my life?" I mutter under my breath, walking towards them. Eric likes me, I like Jason and Jason, well; he seems to be mysterious. Sometimes, I feel he likes me, whenever we are alone he is so different, but the moment Lyra comes into the picture he changes.

"Hey," I say, reaching the car where they are standing.

"What took you so long?" Stella questions me.

"Nothing," I reply.

"So, Casey Dalton..." Eric smiles; speaking my name.

"Yeah," I reply back, faking a smile.

"You are ... beautiful," he adds, sheepishly, and looks at the ground.

Eric seems to be a decent and simple guy. He has a fair complexion, short black cropped hair, adorably cute nose and his eyes; well, the one thing I noticed in a few minutes about him is, he smiles through them. So, if Jason never exists he has a fair chance of winning my heart, but now that I've met Jason, I don't think I am ever going to like any other guy. Ever.

"And you are ... well..." I am about to say something when Stella's cell phone rings loudly. She walks a few steps away, talking to someone over the phone.

"Hey, Eric I need your car," she shouts out, a second later. Eric throws the car keys in her direction and she leaves the school, driving Eric's car in a blink of an eye. I realize that I am alone with Eric. Gosh, why? Now what do I do?

"What's the plan, Dalton?" he questions.

"No plan," I reply.

"Great," he says, smiling ear to ear.

"Huh?" I say confused. My mind is completely exhausted by now; all I want is to sleep.

"Hungry?" he questions.

I simply nod a NO.

"Can I have your car keys?" he asks.

"Why?" I immediately question

"I want you to see something," he says.

I hand over the keys and we walk in the direction of the car. He opens the door for me and I get inside the car. He keeps driving the car and I just close my eyes trying to think nothing, but my mind, it just doesn't obey my orders. The conversation in the Chemistry lab keeps playing in my head and then all I want is to slap myself. How can I ever call him a 'misguided drunken angel'? Well, I know he does look like an angel, but that doesn't mean I should say it on his face. Where did I get all the guts from? I mean the way I acted in front of him seems so alien to me now. I flirted with him. How? The Casey Dalton, I know is a shy girl and not a flirt! Gosh, he is changing me. Thinking about him is exhausting me more so I open my eyes and look around. It is a deserted forest area or whatever.

"Where are we going?" I question a little shocked.

"Just a few minutes," he answers.

"Eric, where are you taking me?" I shout a little.

"Stop spoiling it, please will you?" he replies.

What spoiling? I shouldn't have come with him here; I mean I just met him a few minutes ago. I don't even know him. What does he think of himself?

"Eric, stop the car!" I shout out.

"Case..." Before he can speak something I shout a little more.

"Stop the car!"

He stops the car immediately and says, "Look around."

I look around, it is beautiful. He has brought me to a lake side that is heavenly.

"Sorry," I immediately apologize.

"All cool," he replies.

We get out of the car and start walking towards the lake. The trees are mirrored on the lake water, leaves dancing with the flow of the wind. The water is calm and has so many hues of blue. As we walk ahead and sit on the rocks which are at a distance from the lake, I see small ripples forming on the water surface. It is so cool here, almost cold.

"You like it?" he questions.

"Yeah, it's beautiful and so calm," I reply back, smiling. My mind is almost quiet by now and the view gives me the much needed peace.

"Not as beautiful as you are," he adds.

I can't resist a smile. I look at him and he keeps looking at me, without blinking his eyes. As soon as I see the love screaming in his eyes, I look away.

"How do you find Franklin High?" he says, breaking the silence.

"Well, I didn't expect to make so many friends in so little time. I like it here," I reply, smiling. In the back of my mind I know the real reason behind liking Franklin High; Jason.

"Find anyone interesting so far?" he asks.

"I don't know," I lie. I know it isn't fair to keep him away from the, truth but he is Stella's friend. If he opens his mouth in front of her, I'll be almost dead and secondly I don't really know how he would react to me liking Jason.

"Casey, would you like to go to dinner tomorrow?" he questions.

"I'll think about it and let you know," I reply.

As we see the sun setting, both of us get going towards the car. Eric is a nice guy, he is not confusing, comes straight to the point. But Jason, there is something about him that I can't let go off. I drive Eric home and then come to mine, completely exhausted. One more thought and my mind will blast out.

Chapter 5

I come to my room, feeling exhausted. I get into my sweat pants and try not to bring more thoughts to my mind; but it isn't working. I walk to the washroom, stand in front of the mirror and splash water on my face a few times; trying to erase the thoughts from my mind, making it empty. Yet, it doesn't work. I walk out of the washroom and recline on the bed, closing my eyes. A moment later, I hear my phone buzzing; the screen displays an unknown number.

"Hello?" I say, receiving it.

"Hey, reached home?" The guy on the other end questions; his voice sounds familiar, but my exhausted mind couldn't recollect.

"May I know your name?" I reply, my voice turning off.

"Don't you think it's kind of rude to forget the person who was with you some fifteen minutes ago and also who just showed you one of the most beautiful sights in the city?" he explains, I can sense him smiling and his face pops in front of my eyes; Eric.

"Well, does this change your mind about taking me to the dinner, tomorrow?" I question

"Not really," he replies.

"Okay, see you tomorrow," I say.

"Yeah, good night," he replies.

"Night," I reply and disconnect the line. I close my eyes again, inhaling some air. It is then that I realize what I've actually done; I just invited another problem by saying yes for the dinner tomorrow. I am totally going bonkers now and also that I need a sound sleep.

******

"Casey, Honey..." I hear Jen's voice in my ears.

I open my eyes and sit up straight, still covered with the blanket.

"Hi," I murmur and smile.

"Case, are you all right?" Dad asks, walking inside the room.

"Yeah," I say, nodding.

"I am just a little sleepy," I add, smiling.

"Okay, so let's get you something to eat," Jen suggests.

"No, just some milk would be fine," I reply.

I drink some milk and then both of them kiss me goodnight, turning the lights off. I keep my eyes close until I hear their footsteps fade away. I crack my one eye open and look all around the room; it is dimly lit. The light's probably coming from the night lamp above my bed. There is pin drop silence, like I can hear my heartbeats getting steady and then fading away all at once. Suddenly I feel something inside me, like there is something down at the pit of my stomach. At first I feel it is the puke but no, it is entirely different. It is calm yet desperate; desperate to get hold of something. If only I know what it needs, I will give an end to this sick feeling. The feeling is making me feel dizzy and I feel a sudden need to drink something. It is making me feel thirsty. I immediately turn the lights on and gulp some water from the glass on the side table. I take a deep breath and turn the lights off, getting myself into the bed. A moment later, the feeling is back; this time more desperate and thirsty. I tightly close my eyes; images of Jason and Lyra keep playing in my head making me feel miserable. Something died inside me today, when I'd known that Jason doesn't remember kissing me, when I'd known that they were kissing in the locker room...

"Why did he do this to me? Why?" I whisper, tears rolling down my eyes.

Is it so easy? Am I so easy to forget? Am I? These questions keep haunting me, until I open my eyes. I look at the ceiling; the vision gets blurred with the tears evolving in my eyes. A few days back, my life was normal; simple and then suddenly it gets hit by a storm named "Jason." Besides this, Eric enters my life out of nowhere and I have no idea what's going on in my life.

"Maybe, Eric is your knight in shining armour," My heart whispers. I immediately brush that very thought away and close my eyes.

At night, my heart does return back, although it is damaged but my heart has enough of strength and courage to fight back the demons and find a way back to myself. I can't lose myself in the dark or maybe it is love that has brought me back

******

I wake up with the sound of birds chirping outside the window of my room and it is already past 8 o'clock. I just have fifteen minutes left for school.

"Dad," I shout, coming out of the bed. Well, nobody replies back which means he has already left for work. He just left without waking me up. Wow, my dad is so in love that he is forgetting he has a daughter. I walk down to the kitchen as my tummy makes the dying whale noise out of hunger. I actually want to skip breakfast and have a bath, but my stomach makes me realize that I haven't eaten anything last night. So, unfortunately I'll have to go to school without having a bath. Gosh! That itself is sounding so gross. I quickly make some coffee and scrambled eggs, still wishing somewhere I would get some time to bathe. After, I am done preparing my breakfast; I get all of it down my stomach like a pig and mentally decide what to wear. Later, I rush to my room, wash my face thrice and get into my clothes. I wear a pink colour T-shirt which has the quote on it; 'I cause break-ups' and accompany it with my short denim skirt. Now the problem is my hair, and they are just not settling. Today is undoubtedly one of my bad hair days, so I just clip them up in a half pony and spray a lot of deodorant. I rush to the car, locking the house and drive towards Stella's place.

"I am already feeling so gross!" I mutter under my breath. I usually don't like going out, especially to the school, without bathing and also in my messy hair. All my attempts to impress Jason are in vain now, I look like garbage already. I stop the car; Stella is already waiting outside her house.

"What have you done to your hair?" she questions immediately, after getting in the car.

"I know I look like a gar..." I am about to complete but she interrupts.

"You should get your hair done this way permanently, look at you; you look gorgeous," she says, staring at me.

"Huhh?" I say, confused totally. What gorgeous? I look so gross! I smell like rotten meat.

"I like you this way more, messy hair makes you look sexy!" she says, naughtily.

"Sexy?" I question, shocked.

"Yeah," she replies, typing something on her phone. I am looking Sexy! That's impossible. But what if I actually do? Does she mean I am looking like a slut? No way.

"Hey, you mean this sexy which way, am I looking like a slut?" I blurt out, out of curiosity.

"No. You look sexy in a good way, like a combination of cute and sexy," she explains, robotically.

I smile at her. In the back of my mind I am still thinking whether there actually exists a combination of cute and sexy. I park the car and take a look at myself in the rear view mirror, I kind of look okay but no, not sexy. I am kind of praying in my mind that Jason or Eric, both of them shouldn't be able to see me today or if possible make me invisible to them. Any of the above options are okay. I check my schedule and the first class is Algebra, duh! The thought of solving sums makes me sleepy already. I shouldn't have actually come to school today. I walk to the class and search an empty chair; I have no mood to entertain anyone especially when I am looking a mess. Finally my eyes meet the last chair which is empty and also an opportunity for naps. I quickly make a secret race to it and get my ass settled. I am halfway yawning when my eyes fall on Jason entering the class. He saunters forward in my direction and I can't get my eyes off him. I shake my head down when I realize I've been looking at him with my mouth half open.

"Hey," he says, sitting on the chair next to mine. Wow! I look perfect every day, and he comes to sit beside me when I look all messy. God, you are really great.

"Hi," I say, with my head still down.

"Is there a problem?" he questions.

"No, no..." I reply, looking at him. He is so charming!

"You look different, again," he says, observing me with his dark emerald eyes. I just smile back feeling awkward.

"Your hair..." Before he completes I interrupt.

"Just a bad hair day," I say.

"Well, I think you should have a bad hair day, every day," he remarks.

I look at him startled, but inside I am smiling. Stella was right after all.

"Huhh?" I say pretending.

"Ah, you look kind of ... umm ... good today," he tries to explain, rolling his eyes.

"Thanks," I reply, giving a half smile. I know that his 'good' means sexxxy. Well, he can't get his eyes off me for once. In the meanwhile Mr Anderson enters the class and starts with the new sums. He explains us the method and allots five sums to be done immediately. Well, I frankly don't remember any of the techniques for the obvious reasons; 1) Because, the Greek God is sitting beside me and 2) Because I am sitting beside my Greek God.

"Hey Jason," I call him and see that he's started already.

"Yeah," he replies, looking in my eyes.

"You know how to solve any of these?" I question him.

"He just explained us. What were you doing then?" he questions.

"Well, I was lost in my dream world, now can you help me before he throws me out of the class," I reply.

He nods lightly and explains me the method, well my Greek God is an excellent tutor. After he explains it to me I try solving all of them, but I doubt the last one. I look up at my Greek God and find him already looking back at me. I can't stop myself from blushing.

"What's the answer of the fifth sum?" I question him, immediately.

"Five X raised to two," he says.

I look at the sum again and try to rectify my mistake, but I can't. A second later, Jason shifts my notebook near him and while doing so he touches my hand.

"Here, see you haven't multiplied it correctly," he explains to me my mistake.

"Thanks, I am such a dumbo," I say, solving the sum again.

"That you sure are," he says, laughing it out.

"Haha!" I look at him, making a face.

"Look at you," he says, laughing loudly.

I completely ignore him and solve my sum, pretending to be angry with him.

"Casey," he calls out my name. I do not reply.

"Case..." he calls out again. I keep solving my sum without reacting to any of this. A second later, he snatches my notebook away. Our eyes meet for a brief second, when I look at him. He really has beautiful eyes, the ones where you get yourself lost in and I sure do every time I look him in the eye.

"I am sorry," he says and his eyes have a tinge of sadness in them.

"That's okay," I reply, smiling my best smile. He smiles this time with his eyes and looks at me for a while.

"Stop looking at me." I say.

"Why?" he questions smiling a little.

"I don't know," I reply and look away.

"Casey, you know what?" he adds.

"What?" I ask looking in his eyes.

"You really are a dumbo, but the cutest one of all," he says, smiling. It is hard not to smile back. I wish for the time to stop for a while, but unfortunately the class gets over. I walk to my next class which is Literature with a big smile on my face. When your day starts with the guy you have a big crush on, the day is about to go well. Also he finds me cute. I enter the Literature class wearing a big smile on my face which came from the source I'd spent the past forty-five minutes with. It's weird how he makes me smile without any specific reason. I find Stella sitting on the second last chair and the adjacent chair is empty so I quickly make my way towards it. I am happy and sad at the same time; happy because I have Stella and sad because now I wouldn't be able to sleep in the Literature class.

"Hey," I say, smiling.

"Why didn't you tell me Literature is your second class?" she asked.

"Well, only if I knew it," I say and laugh it off.

Mrs Clark enters the class and I see some kind of sheets in her hand. Later, she distributes them to each one of us and starts writing something on the board.

"Hey Case, do you like Eric?" Stella whispers.

"I don't know yet," I whisper back.

"You don't?" she replies making a face which clearly says that she wants me to like him. Well, he is nice and maybe cute, but he doesn't succeed to get Jason out of my head.

"I think he is cute but I need to know him more," I add.

"You find him cute?" she questions with a naughty smile.

I just half smile feeling awkward. I so want to tell her that I like Jason and that Eric and I, can never be together the way she wants. I so want to tell her, but telling her would be more of a suicide. She just won't understand any of it.

"Casey," she calls me out a little louder and Mrs Clark shoots a stern look at us and we know one more noise from our side and we are sure gonna get thrown out of the class. Mrs Clark lists a few things on the board; Noise, Fire, Wind, Touch. We have to write 1500 words on any of them. I purse my lips, exchange a smile with Stella and choose to write on Noise. I start writing about the noise of ice break in Alaska. I don't even come to know when the class gets over; it is only when Mrs Clark starts collecting the assignments.

"Casey, I feel you and Eric..." Stella starts speaking immediately after the class is dismissed.

"Stella!" I interrupt.

"I need time and till then I don't want to discuss things about Eric, okay?" I say firmly.

"Okay. Fine." She makes a face and bids me goodbye.

The next class I have is Bio; the name itself sets me off to sleep. I am super happy when Mr Mathews enters the class with his laptop. It clearly means he is going show a PPT which also means I can doze off for some time. I hold my head in my hands and move a little forward on the bench; pretending to be interested in the class. As soon as the light is turned off, my mind starts lingering from Jason to Eric, from Eric to Stella and then back to Jason. His face keeps flashing in my mind; it is as if my mind has built a secret banner without taking my permission. The way he was watching me today in the Algebra class keeps bothering me and with this there follows a chain of thoughts. For how long did he observe me? Did I look good while solving the sums? Did I? What was he looking at?? Well, the thoughts never end. Jason has penetrated into me completely. It is as if the moment I am alone or free he will pop up in my head and I can hear his velvety voice calling out my name. The class is over while I keep recollecting all our conversations; even the kiss and then suddenly I am excited to see him again, as it is break.

"Hey," I wave to everyone at the table.

"Dude, why were you smiling in the Biology class?" Zac questions me.

For a second I am like OMG! How could have I not noticed him. This is serious now, I need to get out of my world or else people are gonna conclude that I have gone completely bonkers.

"Me?" I pretend to be innocent.

"Yeah," he says.

"She is happy because her Dad is getting married." Stella interrupts and saves my ass. I know she will be thinking that the smile is because of Eric, but only if she knows the right person behind it. I wish she knew. I get my cheese sandwich, orange juice and start munching it. A second later he enters the cafeteria, I love the way he walks, hands in his pockets and with that expression on his face. Who wouldn't want him? Who wouldn't? Lyra follows him like a shadow and smile at all of us. I expect that Jason will kiss her or maybe she will kiss him but no. Today they are a little away from each other; at least their bodies aren't touching each other. Jason keep stealing glances at me. I check my schedule and butterflies giggle into my stomach as soon as the word Chemistry catches my sight.

I walk to the next class which happens to be a big hurdle between me and the Chemistry class or to be precise Jason. My smile gets wider when I realize that every Friday is a bonus day for me, I am going to have two classes with my Greek God. I happen to reach the Social Studies class early and sit in the second row itself. The reason behind sitting in the second row is that I can rush to the Chemistry lab before Jason and I can watch him walk in my direction. I open the book and I feel a tap on my shoulder, it is Eric. I smile at him and he settles on the chair right next to mine. Before we exchange words Mr Andrews and other students enter the class. The students also include Jason, I want to scream; I love Fridays! As expected, Jason sits on the chair which is on the left to mine. Mr Andrews announces that he is going to show us a movie on err...something. I am so delighted that I don't even listen what the Mr Andrews is saying. He plays the movie and shifts on the last empty chair. A minute later Eric slides a note on my chair. It says,

Is the dinner plan still on? ☺

Yes!

I look at him, he is scribbling something on the same note and look at the Mr Andrews; he is busy correcting something. In the meanwhile, Eric slides the note back, it says,

Excited!!!!

It makes me smile and while writing back to him I sense Jason moving a little awkwardly. I pretend to write and watch him from the corner of my eye, he seems curious to know about the note Eric and I exchanged. I slide back the note to Eric,

Stop being so adorable!

Am I adorable?

Yes and cute too

Well, I know I am kind of flirting around, but I have a plan in my mind which I am sure will make Jason's feelings clearer. And also I didn't lie about any of the above; Eric is adorable and cute though nothing in comparison with my Greek God.

Thank you and you are looking-sexy beautiful today. :P

Sometimes it's okay to be sexy! :P

Okay. You are looking sexy today! ☺

He slides the note back to me and smiles at me. I smile and keep the note on the bench, desperately waiting for the class to get over. The credits roll off and Mr Andrews switches the TV off. I glance at the watch; it is time. The bell rings immediately after that, Eric waits for me until I keep the book into my backpack. I glance at Jason from the corner of my eye and very cleverly drop the note on the floor. The moment the note slips off my hand I get up from my chair and head ahead with Eric. Eric bids me goodbye and I walk to our section in the Lab. My eyes are glued to the door; my heartbeats increasing with every passing second. He enters the lab with Mr Smith, his hands in his jeans pockets. He should be a model, I am telling you. He walks towards me, smiling.

"Why is he smiling?" I ask myself. His smile makes me dead. His smile means he hasn't read the note; he didn't. This is totally unacceptable. Back in the class his body language signalled he was curious. Why God, why? Why didn't you make him read the note?

"Hi again," he says.

"Hey," I reply, smiling my best smile.

"Here, you dropped this back in the class," he said, removing the note from the pocket and placing it on the platform.

WHAT? He read it? HE.READ.IT. Yay! I want to dance, he read the note. He was noticing me in the class; he read it and also brought it back to me.

"Thanks," I say, taking it away and keep it safely in my bag, not that I want to, but it is the best way to make him jealous.

"Everyone, open experiment number three," Mr Smith announces.

I quickly turn the pages ahead and read the title Composition of Compounds. We are instructed to burn copper sulphate, magnesium and carbonate hydroxide. All of us start the experiment as per the instructions given in the journal and simultaneously watch Mr Smith perform. In a matter of minutes we have the chemicals ready in the test tubes and I am all set to hit the burner. I place the burner in front of me and try to light it up, but for some reason it just won't. I try it again, but no, it seems it would never light up.

"Here, let me help you," Jason suggests, trying to take it away.

"No, let me try it one more time," I say, taking it away from him.

"Casey..." His voice gets firm now and I almost feel his breath on my ear. I look at him and the same time I feel a burning sensation in my hand. I immediately break the eye contact as my attention gets diverted to the pain. The burner did light up in the end and with that I burned a part of my palm. The moment I get back to reality, the actual pain sets in and tears escape my eyes. My palm has turned all red by now. Jason immediately walks me to the sick room.

"I told you, didn't I?" He shouts a little.

"It wasn't my fault," I shout back.

"Does it hurt too much?" he questions, as I sit on the bed.

I just nod and we both look for the nurse, but she is nowhere. He takes my hand in his and watches it carefully, making sure he doesn't hurt me in any way.

"It's entirely my fault, I shouldn't have let you do it on your own," he whispers, blowing air on the burn. Goosebumps run through my spine. He looks so innocent, watching my burn and blowing his cool breath on it. His dark emerald eyes clearly screams that he cares for me; more than I ever imagined. He looks around and then says,

"Sit here and don't move, okay?"

"Okay," I quickly reply.

I watch him move inside the room and within seconds he comes back to me, with an icepack and an ointment. He takes my hand into his and softly keeps the icepack on the burn; moving over it.

"Does it hurt?" he questions, looking in my eyes.

Well, if he keeps looking at me the way he is looking right now I will forget who I am, let alone the burn.

"Casey," he calls my name.

"Yeah," I reply looking in his eyes.

"Why are you so stubborn?" he questions, smiling a little.

"I am sorry," I say, looking at the burn.

"You are sorry for what, burning your hand? You are unbelievable," he says laughing.

"Huh?" I can't get the reason behind his laughter.

"I told you already to hand over the burner to me, why can't you just do as I say," he says and I can sense the anger in his voice. I don't know what to reply; well to be quiet is the best thing in such situations.

"Look now, what you have done." He taunts.

"Jason, I am fine. Why are you making it a huge thing?" I reply.

"Seriously, just have a look at it," he says, lifting the icepack.

"It's not that bad, I'll be fine." I lie.

"Well, I guess you should go and get your big eyes checked once," he remarks.

"I do not have big eyes," I say, making a face.

"Yes, you do," he says, looking into them, but I can't see him clearly as my vision gets blurred due to the tears that emerge in my eyes, because of the pain.

"And I can also see how much it is hurting you," he whispers, coming closer.

My heartbeats immediately speed up and I wish very badly that he doesn't come to know about them. He keeps the icepack aside and applies the ointment on the burn, later covering it with a white bandage.

"Thanks," I say, as he leaves my hand. No sooner his touch separates from my skin than I feel the actual pain set in. It does really hurt badly. If I were alone I am sure I will be screaming right now. Jason keeps watching me all this while, well, he does care about me. A tear escape my eye, out of happiness. He wipes it away immediately and cups my face in his hands. For a nano second I think he may kiss me right away but no, he doesn't. I look up at him and then I am lost in his eyes. I am in a complete different world now. It's crazy what he does to me.

"Case, stay away from the things that will destroy you. You are fragile and so is your heart," he murmurs and I smile out of reason. I don't even remember exactly what he told, but whatever it is it sounds nice. He comes closer and I freeze that very moment. He strokes my hair lightly and plants a peck on my forehead. His lips are soft and cold.

"Take care of yourself," he adds and walks away. Now why did he go away? I come out from my dream world and then I am completely tangled. "Case, stay away from the things that will destroy you. You are fragile and so is your heart." His words keep repeating in my mind. What does he mean by that? What is destroying me? I am not fragile? Well, a little. God, this Jason is becoming a mystery now. I mean, every time I feel I have untangled things between us, *BANG* he becomes more confusing. I need to ask him, what he actually meant, but I also know that he wouldn't just answer me straight! The only thing that I know is, he cares about me so, maybe burning my other palm may get me the answer of what he meant by the words he used a few minutes ago. Aargh! I just hope by the time I get to know he loves me I don't completely turn to ash.

Chapter 6

The sound of the bell breaks the chain of my thoughts. I brush all of them away and clear my head, walking out of the sick room. As I start walking towards the Chemistry lab to get my bag, I meet Eric on the way.

"You okay?" he questions, tension mounting on his face.

"Yeah," I reply, faking a smile. I am not okay. I am tangled completely into my Greek God.

"Good Lord, I was so worried," he adds.

"I am completely all right," I assure him.

He smiles back and I can completely make out that he is really happy to find me okay. We start walking in the direction of the lab without exchanging any word. I am feeling so awkward. As soon as we are about to enter the lab someone calls out his name.

"I'll just get my stuff," I tell him and walk inside the lab. I quickly walk to my section and put the journal inside my bag. After packing my stuff, I look around, take a deep breath and walk out of the lab. I look at Eric while coming out of the lab and to my surprise he is talking to Jason. Jason steals a quick glance at me and mumbles something to Eric. I pace my walk, my ears focus on their talk, but before I can listen anything from their conversation, he bids Eric goodbye and walks away. Weird. Super weird.

"Hey," I say smiling, as Eric turns towards me.

"Do you want me to hold your bag?" he questions.

"Eric, for one last time; I am completely all right," I assure him.

"Okay," he says smiling sheepishly. We start walking in the direction of the cafeteria when he suddenly questions,

"You really think I am cute?"

"Well, why would you ask that, don't you trust me?" I say puzzled.

"No, I do. It's just I can't believe you find me cute," he adds.

"What do you mean by that?" I say smiling, inside I want to chuck this baseless topic, find Jason and ask him to answer all my questions, but instead I am stuck with Eric.

"Okay, look... Casey you really matter to me. It's like whatever you do or say affects me in a way..." He was stammering. Oh boy, he really is in love with me. I need to tell him the truth ASAP!

"Eric, Eric," I almost shout at him to make him stop.

"Sorry," he says, looking down.

"I understand what you mean to say, but I don't think school is an appropriate place to talk about what you feel and so, we will talk it out tonight. Okay?" I explain to him.

He nods silently, still looking down at the floor and I feel like hitting myself for hurting him.

"Hey Eric," I call out to him, trying to make him smile.

"What?" he says, looking at me.

"You really are cute," I add immediately, looking in his eye.

Well, looking into these tiny black eyes which keep screaming the love he has for me, doesn't make me feel nervous. I feel nothing. I am all myself, but whenever I look into Jason's eyes, I feel nervous and conscious and scared; scared that his eyes may find out the flaws in my soul and would never want to look back at me. The way his eyes keep searching something into mine; into my soul, it makes me feel different. The thought itself of his gaze meeting mine makes me nervous. As soon as I realize that I am looking at Eric and not at my Greek God, I immediately blink my eyes and look away from his.

"Hey," Stella comes out of nowhere, shoots a naughty look at me and greets both of us. Thank God! I silently pray in my mind, I know she will be thinking that Eric and I are hitting it off together but soon I am gonna let her out of her fantasy world. SOON!

"How is your hand?" she questions me.

Before I answer Eric interrupts, "I'll catch you both in a minute," and walks away.

"Does it hurt?" Stella questions.

"What?" I reply, looking around. Trying to get a glimpse of my Greek God but no, he seems nowhere around me.

"Your hand!" Stella shouts a little, taking my hand in hers. The same time I see Jason and Lyra passing by us and he keeps looking at me for a while.

"No, I am fine now. It doesn't hurt much," I reply to Stella, but keep looking at him. He smiles at me and then we join Zac, Jessica and Mark on our table.

"How's your hand?" Jessica questions me.

"Well, things spread quite fast around here," I remark.

"I am fine now, just a little burn," I add.

"Take care," Mark says and walks away with Jessica. Zac and

Stella are buried in their phones when Eric joins us, sitting beside me.

"I'll pick you up around 8, is that okay?" he murmurs.

"Okay," I reply smiling.

"Where are we going?" I question him.

"Surprise, Surprise," he says, smiling. Stella, Eric and I, move towards the parking lot bidding goodbye to Zac. Stella is probably talking to Kevin so Eric and I keep walking in complete silence. He seems nervous whereas I don't really know what to talk about. He walks us to my car and says,

"Bye and take care of your hand."

"Thanks, bye," I reply, smiling. He smiles back, no he is blushing! Stella bids him a silent bye as she is over the phone. I wait until he turns to walk away.

"What's going on?" Stella questions me, opening the door.

"He is taking me on..." Before I complete my sentence she interrupts.

"He is taking you on a date?"

"No not really. It's just dinner," I say, making things clear.

"Same thing!" she says, with a big smile.

"Whatever," I say because I know she won't understand the difference between a date and a normal friendly dinner.

"That's really sweet of him. Where is he taking you?"

"Surprise, Surprise," I reply, mimicking Eric.

"Have fun, you two. He is really a nice guy," she remarks.

"I know, right," I reply.

"So, what are you planning to wear?" she questions, excited like a child.

"No idea," I reply, killing her excitement.

"Umm, wear a nice dress, not too short not too long. And dare you touch your hair, just let them be the way they are. Okay?" she explains, which sounds more like an order.

"Okay," I reply looking out of the window.

"Why are you so obsessed with my hair?" I add, changing the gear.

She rolls her eyes and replies, "That, is really difficult to answer. I don't know."

"Wow!" I say, laughing.

"Anything else, you want me to do?" I ask her.

"Yes, which flavour lip gloss do you wear?" she enquires.

"Now why are you asking me this?" I ask.

"Umm, wear the one which tastes sweet tonight," she replies, biting her lip.

"Okay, but why are you asking me this in the first place?" I shout a little.

"Miss Casey Dalton, you are gonna have your first real kiss today," she answers.

"What?" I almost choke out. Is she mad? I cannot kiss Eric. No. Never! And just for the matter of fact I had my first real kiss with my Greek God, already and it was well, out of the world.

"Stop acting like a child, already!" she shouts

"Sorry, I got it," I say and end this baseless conversation. How can she even think I would kiss Eric? I don't know him in the first place, let alone the fact that I love Jason. I stop the car near her house and bid her goodbye. She wishes me good luck and tells me that choosing Eric is the best decision I have ever made. Really? I want to ask her, but instead I keep shut. I drive myself home and the first thing that comes to my mind is Susan. I need to tell her everything ASAP. I drink some water and dial Susan's number.

"Guess what??" I say.

"Jason broke up with his girlfriend?" she replies, sounding excited.

"No!" I bark "Dad's getting married to Jen!" I add.

"What? Oh My Gosh!" she replies.

"Yes, it's unbelievable," I say.

"When did all of this happen?" she questions

"Yesterday, quite a day it was," I answer.

"Give me all the details, now!" she screams out of happiness.

"Well, Jen had applied for a transfer when she came to know about Dad's and shifted here. Actually Jen proposed to Dad but he waited for my answer. After discussing it with me, he proposed to her back," I explain.

"Wow!" she remarks.

"Yeah, he is happy and besides Jen is perfect for him," I add.

"This is so amazing; I am excited for the wedding," she shouts

"Yes, it is," I reply.

"What is it Case? Why are you sounding so weird?" she immediately questions.

"I am so screwed up," I mutter

"Aren't you happy with the wedding??" she adds.

"No, I am really very happy about it but..." I break midway.

"But what Case?" she adds.

"There are a lot of things going on together and I am so absofuckinlutely confused!" I shout a little, frustrated.

"Okay, now you do sound screwed up." she replies.

"Wanna talk it out?" she asks. Now that's the best thing about Susan, she never forces me to discuss things.

"Okay, but promise me you are not going to interfere while I tell you everything, promise?" I say.

"Yeah, promise," she replies and I can feel her smile.

"The day Jen proposed to Dad, he took her out for dinner and I went to this nearby church. It was really dark and..." I take a pause.

"What? Someone tried to..." Susan interferes.

"No." I immediately reply.

"As I was walking back home, I met Jason on the way and he was drunk," I add.

"Okay," she replies.

"We had a small conversation and he had this friend along with him who was also drunk, but by the time I was about to leave, his friend disappeared. So, I ask him for his address but..." I stop framing a sentence in my mind about the kiss.

"But??" Susan asks.

"But, he kissed me. I mean we kissed," I mutter as fast as I can.

"Woah! How was it?" she asks, all excited.

"Well, it kind of freaked me out. I was so lost into him," I say, blushing.

"So why are you confused?" she questions

"He was drunk Susan, he has a girlfriend. It's wrong." I tell her.

"Whatever, I am happy that you kissed him!" she laughs

"Technically, he kissed me!" I correct her.

"The story doesn't end here," I add.

"What next?" she asks, naughtily.

"It was too late and he was in no mood to tell me his address, so I brought him home and..."

Before I complete she interrupts, "You lost your V??"

"No!" I shout

"I still can't believe you kissed him." she adds.

"Well, he was watching me like a kid watches a chocolate bar and it just happened..." I try to explain to her.

"No, I mean I am happy!" she shouts and I bet the neighbours can hear her.

I tell her ahead about how he left the rose for me and the note and also how angelic he looked while he was asleep. She too is shocked when I tell her that Jason doesn't remember any of these besides waking up at my place and how he reacts when we are alone. I also tell her about today's Chemistry class, the way he took care of me in the sick room. Also, about Eric and that we are going for dinner tonight. By the time I give her every detail she is all confused with the feelings of my Greek God and suggests to share my true feelings with Eric. I eat some cookies after we hang up and decide that I will tell Eric about my feelings for

Jason. I check the time; 5:35 p.m. There is still plenty of time for dinner, so I decide to take a nap. I lay on the couch, setting an alarm and keep framing in my mind how am I supposed to explain to Eric.

******

I hear my phone ringing. I crack my one eye open and see the screen. It flashes Susan,

"Sussssaaaannn," I say, stretching her name and close my eyes.

"Wake up, sleepy ass," she says from the other line.

"I slept just five minutes ago," I mumble

"Well, it's quarter to 8 already!" she says.

"What?" I immediately jump out of the couch and check the time. Phew! It is quarter to 7.

"Liar!" I bark

"Hahaha..." she laughs on the other line.

"Bitch!" I scream laughing.

"I hope you remember you are going on a dinner date with Eric," she says.

"Yes, I do," I reply.

"Well, then get ready for your next kiss, baby," she teases me.

"I am not going to kiss anyone," I mutter, making a dead-pan face.

"How is Daniel?" I ask.

"Perfect," she replies.

"By the way, I have a plan," she adds.

"What plan?" I ask, yawning.

"You want to find out what exactly Jason feels for you, right?" she asks.

"Yeah, I want to know," I say, his image popping in my head.

"So, I have got a plan for this. You told me he acts indifferent always, like you can't guess what he actually feels..." she pauses.

"Yes," I reply.

"Well in that case let's make him taste his own medicine," she adds.

"Susan, I am not getting what you're saying," I reply, scratching my head lightly.

"What I mean is, if he is giving you mixed signals you too give him back and make him feel the same," she explains.

"I'll try that but I don't really know how I am supposed to make him feel the same," I say, confused.

"Just go with the flow, if he flirts, flirt back. It's as simple as this," she says.

"Okay," I respond half-heartedly because I know it's not that simple.

"Hey Daniel's call is on the line. I'll call you back at night," she says.

"Okay," I reply, walking to the kitchen.

"And have fun. Love you," she says and hangs up.

I make some coffee and come back to the couch with my coffee mug. I look at the bandage wrapped around my palm. Thankfully it doesn't hurt much so, I try to decode the meaning behind his words,

"Case, stay away from the things that will destroy you. You are fragile and so is your heart." I whisper, but it is as difficult as understanding my Greek God. Smile glued to my face, I keep recollecting our conversation and his dark emerald eyes. I hear my phone ringing again.

"Yes Dad," I say receiving the call.

"I'll be late honey," he informs.

"Okay, so are you going to have dinner?" I question him, sipping the coffee. The word dinner makes me realize I am going out with Eric and yet haven't informed dad.

"No," he replies.

"Dad, I..." I pause for a second.

"What? Is it about a guy?" he interrupts immediately.

"Yeah, kind of," I reply.

"I am going out for dinner with a friend," I add, quickly.

"And may I know his name?" he asks and I can feel him smile.

"Eric," I answer, feeling awkward.

"Okay, then have fun on your date," he says.

"Dad!" I almost shout.

"What!" he says mimicking me.

"Bye. Love you," I say and cut the line.

I walk to my room, run the tap of the bath tub and open my wardrobe. I quickly remove the first thing I see; a dress. Tying my hair into a bun, I walk to the bath tub and rest myself in it. The only thing that goes in my mind is how I am supposed to answer Dad's questions tonight. I am sure he will be thinking that I like Eric and all stupid stuff, but the fact is I don't and I have no idea of how to explain everything to him.

"SHIT! I am so screwed up," I mutter, coming out of the bath tub. Walking to the bed, I get the dress over me; it is simple and elegant. The colour is royal blue and ends around my knees; it is tight and fits well until my chest and then opens into a skirt. The dress is also accompanied with a thin leather belt above my waist. All in all I look pretty. I let my hair loose, they seem messier now. I quickly part them apart and make a little puff on the right side, clipping it in a small pin. It is quarter to 8 and I am almost ready. I apply a tinge of lip gloss on my lips, I don't know why, but somewhere in the back of my mind I have this feeling I am going to meet Jason. I have this small voice inside me, which keeps reminding me of Jason.

******

The doorbell rings and I immediately walk towards the door. I take a deep breath and open the door. Eric is here with a bunch of red and white roses, wearing a black shirt and light blue jeans. His hair all settled and I guess he has freshly shaved; well he looks nice; handsome.

"Wow," he says, looking amazed. I smile at him out of awkwardness.

"You look amazing," he adds.

"Thank you," I reply, pretending to blush.

"Hey, did you shave?" I ask him, giggling. He smiles sheepishly and I take it as a yes.

"Well, you look all nice and smooth and ... handsome," I add. He deserves a little buttering; after all I am going to tell him the truth today and besides he does look handsome.

"How is your hand?" he questions.

"The burning has reduced, I'll be fine in a day or two," I respond.

"Shall we?" he questions.

"Yeah, just a second," I tell him and walk inside the house to check if everything is okay.. I close the door behind, collecting my purse and cell phone while he patiently eyes me doing all of this. We walk to the car while he opens the door for me and drives us to the "surprise surprise" as he calls it. We don't exchange a single word except when he hands me the roses that he's brought.

"So, where are we going?" I ask out of boredom.

"Casey, don't be a spoiler now, just a few more minutes," he replies.

"Okay," I reply. He stops the car after we enter the parking and I guess we enter from the back side of whatever place this is. He stops the car and quickly walks around opening the door for me.

"Thank you," I say, coming out of the car. I look around; we are near the pool side of the restaurant named, "Dine and Wine". Well the view is beautiful and dimly lit. There are few tables around the pool side and also some small bulb like things hanging from god knows where all around the area like fireflies. That is it. I need to tell him about my feelings; now!

"You like it?" he asks.

"I love it," I say, looking all around.

"But..." I add and suddenly stop framing a sentence in my head.

"But," he asks.

"If you don't like the place we can go somewhere else ... wherever you want to?" he adds.

"No, it's not about the place, Eric," I say.

"Then," he says.

"Will you please tell me what's going on in your mind?" he adds and I sense the tension in his voice.

"Nothing, let's just go," I say, looking around. I can't tell him today, I mean he has done all this and I can't spoil all of this. He will be really really hurt. God, why did I ever tell him yes for dinner! I am such a bitch!

"I am not going anywhere, until you tell me!" he shouts a little, like a small stubborn child. I look at him, but he doesn't seem to be any mood to negotiate things.

"Now!" he adds.

"Look, I don't want to hurt you..." I say and pause.

"Ms Casey Dalton, can we get straight to the point?" he says.

"Fine. I like you, but only as a friend and I think..." I stop immediately; I just don't have the courage to tell him on his face.

"And?" he asks.

"And I think I love ... Jason and I feel he has something for me," I say these words as fast as possible.

A second later, I look at him; he has this tiny grin forming on his face. I can't understand his behaviour now.

"Eric, you okay?" I question him, a little scared.

"Wow!" he replies.

"I am so sorry," I apologize immediately.

"What are you sorry for?" he questions.

"Well, I kind of..." I run out of words.

"But what's wrong with you?" I ask him.

"Well, now I am sure he has something for you," he answers.

"What?" I say shocked.

"I met him out near the Chemistry lab and we were generally discussing about our football practice when out of nowhere he started talking about this restaurant," he explains.

"So, just because he talked about the same restaurant it doesn't mean he is interested in me..." I tell him.

"Woah! Wait a minute!" I shout.

"He read our note which I'd forgotten, back in the class and..." Before I complete Eric interrupts.

"Bulls eye! He knew I was taking you for dinner and that's the reason he planted this restaurant in my mind," he says. I am smiling my best hearing all of this and suddenly Eric hugs me tightly.

"He is so screwed up," he whispers in my ears.

"What?" I say, confused.

"He is here with Lyra. We were fucking right about his plan," he whispers.

"Now what do we do?" I reply.

"Just keep pretending you like me too much and let's see what happens next," he says. I hug him back making sure it is visible to him.

"Is he looking here?" I ask him.

"Yeah, the game is on," he says, smiling.

"This is going to be super fun," I say, smiling naughtily. As soon as Eric and I part ourselves apart,

"Hey, love birds," Lyra calls out, walking in our direction with Jason. I pretend to look at both of them, but my eyes were lost into Jason's. He looks dazzling, in that white shirt and his worn out jeans. He looks effortlessly charming, not that he needs any efforts to make my heart skip a beat.

"Hey," I say, smiling at both of them and I see Jason smile, but his eyes don't. I guess the plan is working.

"See you around," I tell them, take Eric's hand in mine and signal Eric to walk in the direction of our table.

"Nice move," he says.

"I know right," I reply, smiling. We reach our table; it is beautifully decorated with roses and lilacs. He pulls the chair for me and sits opposite to mine.

"Can you see them?" I question, curiously.

"Yeah," he says, smiling.

"Jason is talking to the Manager," he adds.

"It seems all the tables are reserved and..." he pauses.

"And?" I ask.

"They are about to leave and I am not going to let the Manager ruin our plan." he says, walking away. I follow him walk to where they are standing and within seconds he walks back with both of them. Wow! He convinced them to dine with us. It is gonna be real fun now.

"I hope you don't mind," Lyra says, sitting beside me.

"Not at all, so long as Eric is around me," I say, faking a smile.

Eric and Jason sit opposite to us and you should take a look at Jason, he is so jealous. He keeps stealing glances at me while I keep checking him out from the corner of my eye.

"You both look great together," Jason says, which sounds more like a taunt.

"Yeah, like kind of cute," Lyra adds.

"Thank you," I reply, pretending to blush.

We order the food; Beer-Braised Chicken and vegetables, Turkey and vegetable hand pies, Swiss N' chicken baked rice, noodle salad and cheeseburger pasta. We chat a little more for a while and all the time I pretend to be in love with Eric. Somewhere, in the back of my mind I am a little scared; what if our plan fails?? Nevertheless, the thoughts disappear as soon as the food arrives. The food is delicious!

Every human has a heart, but it lacks feelings, where some fall in love counting their heartbeats and where some wait for the love that might skip their heartbeat.

Chapter 7

"Thank you," I say, looking in his eyes. He smiles and pushes the lock of hair away.

"Jason," I whisper his name.

"Yeah," he replies, still looking at me.

"Jason," I mumble his name again, smiling at him.

"Yes, Casey." he says, looking in my eyes. Damn, his dark emerald eyes. We keep looking at each other, words do not matter anymore.

******

An hour ago...

We discuss about Chicago and New York and the boys discuss about their football practice and Lyra asks about my hand. Things are going pretty well and we have just finished eating the desert when,

"Drinks anyone?" Lyra says.

"Me," Jason replies, immediately.

"Me too," Eric adds. The word 'drink' makes a shiver run through my spine. I look at Jason, remembering the night when I'd brought him home drunk and also the ... the kiss. He looks back at me the same moment and, for a second I feel that he can hear my thoughts. A moment later, he smiles and I smile back. In the meanwhile Jason signals the waiter to order the drinks.

"Margarita." Lyra orders. Well, I have had a few drinks at family gatherings, but this is different and besides I don't want to ruin our plan by getting drunk. I am clueless. What if I really get drunk and speak the truth right in front of Lyra?

"Four beers," Jason adds and I am scared now. I am just hoping that my Greek God doesn't turn into "the misguided drunken angel" again.

"Make it six and Casey, what would you like?" Eric questions me. I shoot a look at him and he clearly understands what's going in my mind.

"Tequila for the lady," he says and completes the order. I keep shut and try to calm down, but no use. He just ordered Tequila!

"I'll be back in a moment," he tells me and excuses himself.

"Okay," I reply smiling and watch him walk away. Where is he going now? I shouldn't have come here in the first place I curse myself. I hear my cell phone beep, it is Eric.

Stop thinking, i have replaced your drink already, just act drunk and let's see how Jason reacts!☺

Phew! He is such a sweet heart. We chat for a little while; Lyra never seems to miss a chance to kiss Jason and I so want to punch her in the face. The drinks arrive and I immediately take mine in my hand, before anybody finds out what it really is. I look at my drink and take a sip hesitantly. Wow! It is water; I want to laugh out loud. I gulp all of it.

"Woah, that was quick," Jason remarks. I smile awkwardly not knowing what to answer. I look around, Lyra is drinking her margarita, Jason has already finished two beer pints and Eric; he is looking at me. I smile at him and he smiles back, his best smile so far. Drinks!

"What? Stop looking at me this way." I complain like a child.

"You look like an angel when you're drunk," he says. Okay, I am drunk, how can I forget that. I need to act drunk.

"No, you're my angel," I reply. He smiles, drinking some more, I rest my head on his shoulder, my hand around his arm.

"Aww, you both look so adorable," Lyra says, smiling.

I expect Jason to react or at least say something, but with time he just gets quieter. I observe him, he is busy analyzing something in his beer bottle or I think it is time for 'my misguided drunken angel' to come out. He looks up and meets my gaze through his long eyelashes and smiles at me. I don't smile back, I just can't. The confusion and the complexity that he has been creating don't allow me to smile back, but he keeps looking at me until I force a smile. He looks away just to look back again and this time his gaze penetrates right through my eyes and into my soul. I feel my heart break; my soul getting ripped off inside. I don't know what he does to me. I can't look at him and not get lost into him. I close my eyes tightly trying to escape this feeling.

The moment I close my eyes, I feel nothing. My heart is calm now; helping me to only breathe and not live. The wounds are deeper now; only that the pain has subsided. The pain; it is right there intact, but somehow I am immune to it. It is changing my heart; changing me into something I am never meant to be; someone I have never known. I do not recognize the person I am now and I do not know how to let this go.

"Casey, you okay?" I hear Eric's voice.

I take a deep breath and open my eyes.

"Yeah, just a little tired," I reply, sitting straight.

I steal a glance at Jason; he is typing something on his cell phone. We pay the cheque and start walking towards the parking. Eric pulls my hand and signals me to let Jason and Lyra walk ahead.

"Why are you not acting like you're drunk?" he whispers.

"Because I am not drunk," I giggle.

"Please don't ruin the plan," he requests.

"Okay," I say.

"According to my calculation, Jason is going to drive us home and as your house is across the church lane, you might get some alone time with him," he explains.

"Why will he drive us home?" I ask, confused.

"Because I've punctured my car purposely," he says.

"Okay," I reply, smiling. He is crazy!

"Look, I know this is all crazy, but he knows you're drunk and there are possibilities that he might speak to you about his feelings," he adds.

I just nod inside I am nervous and on top of that I have to act drunk when I am not. We pace our walk and reach Eric's car.

"Damn it!" he shouts, loud enough for Jason to hear.

"Dude, you didn't check your car?" Jason questions.

"I did." Eric says, irritated.

"I'll drop you guys. Is that cool?" Jason adds.

"Yeah, cool," Eric replies.

We get into his car and I remember that I need to act drunk. As soon as everyone settles and Jason starts driving, I start the drama.

"Hey Eric," I say, framing the next sentence in my mind.

"Yes," he replies, looking at me.

"Do you like Dragons?" I ask him. The entire conversation is loud enough for Jason to hear.

"No. Why?" he questions

"What why?" I question back.

"Why are you talking about Dragons, Casey?" he adds.

"Because... they are ... ummm ... Dragons," I say, sounding like a complete idiot, but that's how drunk people talk, right?

"You're drunk Casey," Lyra says, laughing.

"No! I am not drunk!" I bark.

"Yes you are…" she says again, laughing.

"No! I am just haaappppyy!" I reply, stretching the word happy.

"Okay, happiness. Let's just close our eyes and relax," Eric says.

"But I don't want to. I want to talk about Dragons and mermaids and elephants and air conditioner," I reply, making a face.

"No just try once, you will feel better," he insists.

"You know what Eric?" I ask.

"What?" he replies.

"You're a Dinosaur," I say, making a weird face.

The same time, Jason stops the car and Lyra bids us goodbye. I notice Jason doesn't even kiss her goodnight. Now, that is really rude! Anyways, the more he stays away from her the better.

"No, I am not a Dinosaur, you are!" Eric says, shouting a little.

"I am not talking to you. You're very bad," I shoot at him.

"So are you, you're calling me a dinosaur," he replies.

"Because that's what you really are, a dinosaur!" I shout at him, making a face.

The moment I complete my sentence, Jason stops the car. I look around; it doesn't seem like my neighbourhood. So, Eric was right. Eric and I get out of the car when,

"Good night, dinosaur," he says, planting a kiss on my cheek.

"Good night," I reply smiling and I see him walk towards his house.

"You mind sitting ahead?" Jason says, opening the door.

"Okay!" I say, loudly.

In the back of my mind, I want to slap myself tightly for the things I said a while ago. Dinosaurs! Air Conditioner? How did that even come to my mind?

"You sound cute when you're drunk," he says, starting the car.

"And when I am not, I am not cute?" I sigh, making a puppy face.

"Of course you are, but you are not always drunk right? It's kind of fascinating," he answers.

"And you're a dinosaur!" I say, not knowing how drunken people deal with such situations.

"Well, you first need to decide who I am. Am I 'your misguided drunken angel' or am I a dinosaur?" he questions.

Wow! All this while he was quiet and now that we are alone he just can't shut his mouth.

"I don't know," I say, looking out of the window.

"That's okay; I can be anything you want me to be," he responds and I feel him smile.

I know these are just words; empty words. I can never have him the way I want; he'll never be mine. The word 'mine' tortures my heart and I feel suffocated even though fresh air keeps brushing my cheeks. I know I cannot have him but ... but my heart, it just doesn't accept this.

******

"Case," I hear Jason's voice, his cool breath around my ears.

I turn my head and look at him; his face is too close to mine than it should be.

"You okay?" he questions, his eyebrows making a little hill on his forehead.

"Yeah, just a little..." I run out of words when I look in his eyes.

"Casey," he says, and brings me back to reality.

I smile and murmur, "Good night."

"Night," he says, smiling.

"I'll walk you home," he adds.

He opens the door for me and helps me to get out of the car, holding my hand.

"Thank you," I say, looking in his eyes. He smiles back and pushes the lock of hair away.

"Jason," I whisper his name.

"Yeah," he replies, still looking at me.

"Jason," I mumble his name again, smiling at him.

"Yes, Casey." he says, looking in my eyes.

Damn, his dark emerald eyes. We keep looking at each other, words don't matter anymore.

I don't know what he does to me? He is like a magician; whenever he is around I feel my heart dancing in amazement. I wish I can keep him forever; I wish.

My phone beeps and I am brought back to reality. I think it must be Eric or Susan but it is from Dad; *hon, I am with Jen, good night. Love Dad.*

"Eric?" Jason questions and I sense the curiosity in his voice.

"No, it's my Dad. He is with his girlfriend and won't be coming home tonight," I inform. The moment these words slip out of my mouth I pray to God that Jason just doesn't take this the other way around.

"SHIT!" I shout all tensed a second later.

"What's wrong?" he questions.

"I don't have my house keys with me, I mean I had it in my purse and I left it in Eric's car and my Dad is..." I panick completely.

"Casey!" he shouts a little.

"What!" I shout back, thinking what to do.

"Stop it!" He shouts again.

"Stop what!" I bark.

"You're drunk!" he says.

"No, I am not!" I shout and realize I have to act drunk plus this is an opportunity to check what he's going to do when I am all alone and drunk. So, let the game begin!

"I don't know what to do now, I can't go to Stella's place it's too late and I don't want to disturb Dad and Susan, yes I'll go to Susan's place." I keep murmuring.

"Who's Susan?" he questions.

"You don't know whose Susan?" I exclaim.

"No?" he says.

"She is my best friend." I say.

"So, I'll just take you to her place, then," he suggests.

"Okay," I reply.

"Where does Susan live?" he questions.

"Susan's home!" I shout.

He pulls me closer to himself; it is more like snatching myself away from me into him. He cups my face into his hand and murmurs,

"Casey..."

"Hmmm," I reply, smiling.

"Where does this friend of yours live?" he questions.

"Which friend?" I ask, completely lost in his eyes.

"Susan," he says.

"I think she has a house, yes, and you know when we were kids ... we used to play on the paveme..." I am about to complete, but he pulls me closer to himself.

I can't meet his eyes now, I close them, scared. My heart throbbing in my mouth I look down, hoping that he will leave me out of his embrace. A second later, his finger touches my chin and he tilts my face up, meeting his eyes with mine. Within a fraction of seconds, his lips are on mine. My lips dance synchronizing with his and I know it is wrong, but I have no control over it. This time the kiss is different; it isn't that wanting, but instead it makes me feel safe. It is as if he is trying to convey that I am safe with him and he'll never leave me alone. Never.

"I am sorry," he mumbles, near my lips as we part away.

I have a million questions to ask and equal things to say, but instead I remain silent. I don't know why, but even when it's wrong it feels so right. What's wrong with me?

******

"Case, are you okay?" Jason questions me, as I got seated on the couch.

"Yes," I reply.

"Then why are you not speaking anything?" he adds, sitting beside me.

I am actually out of words, I mean, I expected that he would drop me to Stella's or Eric's house, but instead he brought me here; he brought me to his place. I really don't know who he is. Sometimes he is so confusing, sometimes so mysterious, and sometimes so warm towards me and sometimes he is a complete stranger.

"Where are your parents?" I inquire.

He laughs it off and then his expression changes, his face hardens and pain emerges in the eyes of my Greek God.

"I don't know, I guess they are busy in their own lives," he whispers.

"I am sorry," I reply.

"No, what are you sorry for?" he questions

"I shouldn't have asked you," I whisper.

He smiles switches on the dim lights above the couch simultaneously turning the lights off and turns on the television.

"It feels so right to be here, with him and yet it is so wrong." I wonder.

"Casey, you okay?" he questions me again.

"Why are you asking me this again and again?" I ask

"Because, my dinosaur, you have suddenly sealed your mouth." he explains, smiling.

I smile blankly and watch the TV screen, *X Men* series is tuned on HBO. The movie has the scene where the female lead tells the story about the Moon and the kuekuatsheu, but suddenly Jason turns it off. I rest my head on the couch and close my eyes when,

"Why is the moon so lonely?" he murmurs.

I open my eyes and look at him.

"Because she used to have a lover," I reply yawning.

He smiles, caresses my hair and comes closer. I rest my head on his shoulder and he puts his arm around me, securing me into his embrace.

"And also because the lover fears hurting the fragile Moon," he whispers and kisses my forehead. I snuggle inside him a little and close my eyes. My mind is too tired to decode the meanings hidden in his words. I know all this is wrong and I am acting all crazy, but I have no choice, I mean I can't let this moments slip away merely because it seems wrong. I crack open my eyes and see my Greek God resting in sleep. He has this little glow on his face and a small smile glued to his lips. I brush my fingers against his cheek and his hold on me tightens, he pulls me close towards him. I quickly plant a kiss on his forehead and I don't know why, but a second later, my lips brush against his. As soon as I realize that I've kissed him, I quickly hide my head in his chest; embarrassed.

******

I am a dreamer and he is my dream; a breathtakingly beautiful dream. A dream which may never come true but also which no one can take away from me; never. You are a dream; my dream. I can call you mine here and can be yours. You'll always be in my 3am thoughts when in the middle of the night, I'll be awakened with the pain in my heart; pain of not having you and not having the privilege to be called yours. Now, that I'll always have you with me, a part of me; my heart, I'll only stop dreaming of you once life takes my breath away. And I wish one day, I never wake up and lose myself in this dream forever.

******

"Morning Sunshine," he whispers into my ears.

"Mmm," I blabber, coming out of my sleep. I hardly slept last night, I was so conscious in my sleep that it just takes his voice to let me out.

"Hey," I say, opening my eyes, a second later.

Wow! We slept together, like not sleep-sleep but sleeping, if you know what I mean. He looks really beautiful with sleep in his dark emerald eyes and also my reflection in them. I roll my eyes around and notice that I am still secure in his embrace; he didn't even move an inch the entire night.

"What time is it?" I question, when he finally gets up from the couch.

"Quarter to 11, I guess," he answers, walking to the kitchen, finally separating himself from him.

"SHIT!" I blabber. I search for my cell phone panicking a little, but it seems nowhere.

"Jason," I shout his name out.

"What?" he shouts from somewhere inside the kitchen.

"Where is my phone?" I bark.

"Relax! Already informed your Dad," he shoots.

"What? WHAT?" I explode.

"Why are you shouting?" He walks to me and then, my mouth is completely sealed.

He stands there, right in front of me, wearing his sponge-bob square pants boxers and holding two cups of coffee. Where are his clothes?? But leaving this aside he looks truly gorgeous like maybe a cute boxer model. I study his body and see two tiny moles on his collarbone.

"Hey, where did you get these sponge-bob square pants?" I ask him, as I realize I've been observing him too much and I need to speak something.

"Huhh?" he says looking at me and all I do is smile like an idiot. Gosh! How can I even think of having him in my life, when I act so weird in front of him? Spongebob-squarepants boxers, I really need to keep some back up excuses because I sound a little too lame sometimes.

He smiles sheepishly and says, "Why are you shouting so much?"

"Yes, no, I mean what did you tell him?" I suddenly scream, coming out of my thoughts.

"Why did you call my Dad? Are you crazy?" I add, a second later.

"Shit, he must be thinking that you are my boyfriend! SHIT. SHIT. SHIT. And that we slept last night. HOLY COW!" I shout.

"Yeah we did sleep last night, everybody does..." he laughs.

"No, not like sleep-sleep, I mean like ... uh forget it." I sigh.

"Hold on, what are you talking about?" he asks, confused.

A second later, he hands me my cell phone and shows me the text message;

I had forgotten the keys last night so I stayed back at Stella's place. Will be home soon. Love you.

"Thank God." I sigh in relief. I excuse myself to freshen up and just when I walk back to the living room I hear him over the phone,

"Yes Babe," he says.

"Of course I love you, yeah bye," he adds and ends the call.

The moment I hear these words my heart sinks a little. My day dream has turned into a nightmare. I've already started hating myself for doing this to me. Why did I come here in the first place? Regret is creeping all over my heart. He signals me to sit on the couch and I sit next to him all confused.

"Hey, why did you kiss me last night?" I blurt out suddenly. It is enough now, he can't keep playing with my heart always. I want answers.

"What?" he says, almost choking while taking a sip of the coffee.

"Jason, why did you kiss me?" I repeat.

"Because I've recently read somewhere that kissing reduces anxiety and stops the noise in the mind. It increases the levels of oxytocin, an extremely calming hormone, that produces a feeling of peace," he completes.

"I asked you why did you kiss me and not what kissing does to our body!" I shout.

I wait for his answer but he has nothing to say. He is silent.

"Why?" I scream out in pain, tears rolling down my cheek.

"I ... ummm..." That's all he has to say.

"Are you going to tell me why??" I bark.

"Why are you making it such a huge thing?" he shouts.

"You know what, forget it..." I say and burst into tears.

"Yes, that's exactly what I mean. Let's just forget it, you were drunk and it happens all the time..." he says.

"Happens all the time..." I repeat his words in my mind. What does he mean by that? I am not a slut and what happens all the time in his world, has happened to me just twice and he was a part of it.

"Casey, relax. Just calm down," he consoles.

"I am fine and you need not worry about that," I mutter under my teeth and get up from the couch.

"Where are you going?" he questions.

I don't feel the need to answer his question anymore. I start walking back home, closing the door shut behind and hoping that I would never open it again.

Chapter 8

"Honey you okay?" Dad questions me, as soon as I enter the house.

"Yeah, just a little tired," I reply, sitting beside him on the couch.

I am praying inside that he just doesn't shower more questions regarding last night.

"You want me to make something for you, pancakes?" he questions.

"No, I am fine," I say, faking my best smile.

Then I notice that he is all dressed up, maybe going somewhere so I enquire, "Going somewhere?"

"Yeah, to the grocery shop and then Jen is joining us for the lunch," he informs.

"Okay," I say, smiling.

Generally I like to spend my Sundays with Dad, but today I am just not myself. I am relieved after knowing that I am finally going to be alone. I bid Dad goodbye and run upstairs to my room, tears rolling down my cheeks. My heart is wounded, damaged and shattered completely by the one whom I thought would keep me safe; my heart safe.

"Why?" Was the only question in my mind.

"Why he did this to me? Why?" I whisper in my broken voice.

It is as if my nerves have been shaken out of my body and

scattered around the floor, but he seems perfectly fine because he is the one who's been doing it all this while. I am a fool who is trying to find that innocent little child in him, but I am so wrong. People like him never had that innocent little child in them and if they ever did then maybe, just maybe, the child had been murdered long back.

"What was my mistake?" I howl in pain.

I hate him and more than that I hate myself for craving a love so deep for him. I am cursing myself for every single time I've let him look into my eyes, my soul; I've let him make me fall for him. I shouldn't have come here in the first place. I regret every single breath I've taken here. I hate myself for trying to understand him when there is nothing to understand at all. I wish I'd stayed away from him, I wish I'd listened to Stella. I shouldn't have changed myself, just for him to notice me. I'd forgotten that people like me don't fit in this world; fake world. People like me do not belong here because we don't understand to fuck up someone's life when we are tangled in our own. People like me are not meant for love, at least not me because when I love, I love.

I know all this while, I've been running away or not accepting the truth completely, but I am not the one at fault, it's Hope. Every time I decide to accept the truth and walk away from Jason, a new hope sparkles between us. But now, I understand that it isn't Hope but it is Jason. It is his heart which has been playing with mine. My heart is just another toy for him; I am just a toy. And when the bruises on my heart have begun to fade, exactly then, just then he wounded me again. A wound so deep that even the sea might get jealous. But what he doesn't know is that, not all wounds heal and even when they do, they always leave a scar. And he'll always be a scar; the most remarkable and the most painful one.

******

"How was your date?" Dad asks, teasing me.

I almost choke while chewing the pancake in my mouth.

"Cool," I lie, fighting the tears in my eyes.

"And how's Eric?" Jen adds.

"Good," I mutter through my teeth.

"Mm, so do you like him?" Dad adds, sipping his coffee.

"Dad!" I shout, trying to be myself and I am sure they can't make out that I am pretending or lying when all I want to do is cry.

"Dad!" He mimics me and laughs it off.

"It was just a date Dad, I'll let you know if there's anything more to it." I explain to him and end this topic. I am never going to tell them about my 'real date'.

"William!" Jen interferes, while Dad is about to speak something.

"So, we have been thinking to schedule our marriage around Christmas, maybe 22nd, what do you think?" she adds.

"Wow, that's great!" I say, excitedly.

"And we might be honeymooning in Paris!" she informs.

"And 'we' includes you too," Dad interrupts.

"What?" I ask them, shocked.

"You are coming with us!" Jen repeats.

"Was that a joke?" I say, still shocked.

"No!" They both shout together.

"What makes you think, I am interested in your honeymoon?" I ask them.

"We are not leaving you here alone, and moreover it's Christmas!" They both snap together.

"Who says I'll be alone, Susan is going to be at the wedding so, I'll make sure she stays!" I snap back.

"Are you sure?" Dad questions me.

"Yes," I reply.

We finish the lunch, discussing the Marriage and Christmas. Their wedding is scheduled on 22nd December which is after 10 days. I am so happy, for a while I forget about Jason and the pain. Later, I excuse myself because I have to prepare for the tests which are starting from Tuesday. The moment I am in my room, the sick feeling starts penetrating, but Susan helps me escape it.

"Guess what?" I shout, receiving her call.

"What?" she says, from the other end.

"Ms Susan Martin, I hereby, make this official that Mr William Dalton and Ms Jennifer Miles are getting married on 22nd December 2013." I declare.

"That is awesome!" she shouts

"I know right." I reply.

"And guess what else?" I add.

"I am over this guessing thing, please just tell me," she says, in a puppy voice.

"They will be going to Paris for their honeymoon so ... we can celebrate Christmas together, in Chicago." I say.

"And I am thinking to call Daniel over, what say?" she suggests.

"That'd be great!" I reply.

"Woah, I am so excited!" she says.

"So am I," I reply, smiling.

"But now let me ask you the reason for which I have called you, how was your date?" she asks.

"It was great," I lie. In the back of my mind I am struggling between deciding whether to lie or say the truth, but then I just don't feel like telling her everything. Maybe I'll tell her after the wedding, maybe. I have no courage to give her the details she will ask me regarding last night so I have no option, but another lie.

"Hey Susan, you mind if I call you later. I need to study for the tests," I ask.

"That's fine; anyway we are meeting for the wedding. Good luck for your tests," she says and hangs up.

It is strange for the first time in so many years; nobody notices that I am unhappy. It is like they believe whatever I say or they trust me too much. Either way it is good because I don't want to spoil the wedding and moreover lying or faking a smile is better than explaining the truth; which itself is a mystery to me. I just have to keep myself busy with stuff and there I am all okay. So, why not start with the tests. I have nothing to do and thinking about Jason will hurt me more so, I focus on my studies. Back then I always scored good grades, but this time when I have so many distractions I am a little scared.

******

MONDAY: By now I've learned to ignore Jason and the thoughts that make me upset and the memories that hurt. At first, I don't want to go to school, but not going to school means running away from my own feelings. I check the schedule and as soon as my eyes read the word Chemistry, I feel the wound in my heart. I am all ready and pick Stella as usual. On the way we discuss about the date and I lie giving the details and she is happy to know that Eric and I had a great time. I also inform her about the wedding date getting confirmed and then she is all about the dress she will be wearing and suggesting what I should wear and etcetera. We reach school and my first class is Social Studies. I initiate a talk with that geek guy Ethan and it helps. The more I keep talking and focus on the class I feel good. The next two classes are with Stella and time runs faster than I think. By now, the test schedule is put up and the rest of the week we have just tests, isn't that great? I mean I won't be meeting Jason, no Chemistry class, nothing. Our classes would be conducted right after the Christmas break and the winter Prom that I have no plans to attend. But once we have our break and the time till the school re-opens, I'll be healed completely, also I have almost made my mind to go back to New York and I'll even repeat a year if required, but Chicago is a big NO! I glance around for Jason in the break, but he seems nowhere. Later, I have Literature class with Jessica and then it is Chemistry. I think of bunking the class at first, but then I am not going to let Jason feel good about hurting me; to him I am perfectly happy in my life. I've made up mind that I would just ignore him completely even if he looks deliciously cute! But surprisingly, he doesn't turn up. He is nowhere, well, my mind does linger for a few seconds, but then it is all under control. I meet Eric after school and explain to him the details which I told Stella about the date night and he informs that all is cool. School is over without any drama, prom night preparations and tests.

TUESDAY: Today is Algebra and I am sure I'll score an A+ until I see him. Crap! He looks perfect in his grey T-shirt with the words 'Incredible Hulk' and worn out jeans. Well, he sure is incredible, but the word 'Hulk' doesn't suit his personality. I watch him move around the class and he sits right across my seat. Phew! There is an entire row between us. I recollect myself from his "incredible effect" and focus on my test. My eyes are dying to see him again and I can't control myself then. The test doesn't meet my expectations as I will find myself looking at him every once in a while. Finally the time is up and I escape the classroom. I meet everyone and chat for a few minutes, leaving school with Stella. At home, I am struggling back to sleep after preparing for my next test. I am mentally prepared for tomorrow; for him.

WEDNESDAY: Today is Literature and I love this subject so I am all calm. Also, I don't see him today, like I just keep looking down at the floor and then the test sheet or the desk, but not him. I do not even know whether he is there in the class or not; I make him disappear from my mind. As soon as the test is over I rush out of the class and wait for Stella in my car. It is more easy this way, trying to escape helps me a lot. Back at home I am easily asleep as I study until my eyelids are heavy enough to meet each other.

THURSDAY: Today is Biology and I have prepared enough to score an A. I don't see him today as well; just keep looking down at the floor and then the test sheet or the desk. I don't even know whether he is there in the class or not; I make him disappear from my mind. As soon as the test is over I rush out of the class and wait for Stella in my car. It is more easy this way, trying to escape helps me a lot. Back at home I am easily asleep as I study until my eyelids are heavy enough to meet each other.

FRIDAY: Today is Social Studies and I hate this subject, but still I know I'll score a B. I do not see him today too; just keep looking down at the floor and then the test sheet or the desk. I don't even know whether he is there in the class or not; I make him disappear from my mind. As soon as the test is over I rush out of the class and wait for Stella in my car. It is more easy this way, trying to escape helps me a lot. Back at home I can't fall asleep even though my eyelids are heavy enough to meet each other. All these days I've followed a routine, I've been skipping Jason, but tomorrow I'll have to face him. The tests are going to end and Monday is our Prom night. All these days, I'd made a routine to tire myself so much that my mind was left with no energy to think about him, but now that the tests are over; I will need something else to keep myself busy now.

SATURDAY: Today is Chemistry and somehow this subject is close to my heart for the obvious reasons. I know that today is going be different from the rest of the week, but I have no clue that it will be from Jason's end. Unlike the other days, today I see him and to my surprise he looks entirely different. Well, physically he still looks charming and perfect in his navy blue T-shirt and greyish jeans, but there is something different about these dark emerald eyes. They seem reckless and lost. God alone knows how much I wanted to see him and his dark emerald eyes in the past few days. All those days I pretended to be over him, but one look at him and I know I am still that much into him as I am on day one. But besides all this I see him glancing at me almost after every five minutes. Wow, can you believe that? I am hardly able to concentrate as, his eyes on me is a huge distraction and now when I know that he is looking at me I am super conscious. I can't wait for the test to get over and just disappear. I am relieved when the bell rings, but then Mr Andrews announces,

"No one leaves the class."

In the back of my mind it goes, WHAT THE HECK! Well, I can't meet Jason's eyes and let him peep into my soul so; I just bury myself in the Chemistry journal. I try diverting my mind and keep thinking about the marriage, but no use! Jason is all over me and I have that creepy feeling that he is still looking at me. A moment later, Mr Smith enters the class,

"All of you need to submit the Chemistry project on Monday."

SHIT! It can't get worse. Jason and I are partners in the Chemistry project and talking to him means hurting myself again. What do I do? As soon as he leaves, the school President announces in the speaker,

"Attention everyone, choose your partners for the Winter Prom Night to be held on 24th December, 2013"

"FUCK!" I mutter under my breath. I've already made up my mind that I am not going to that shitty prom. All this is so zombie-ish. The class is dismissed as soon as the announcement gets over, but just then someone passes me a note. A glance at the handwriting and I know it is Jason's.

I am sorry for everything and I am going to make it up by helping you in the Chemistry project, meet me whenever you have free time. Heard about your Dad's marriage, congratulations! ☺

His handwriting reminds me of the night we'd kissed and also the rose that I still have hidden in my closet. I look up from the note and search him around, but he is nowhere. AARGH! "I am sorry", that's it! How does he know about the marriage and what makes him even think that I'll be completing the project with him, I'd rather flunk in Chemistry. Enough is Enough! He disappears leaving a note and expects me to chase him all the way, no. Never. I do not need him and moreover I don't need his help in the project. Instead I am happy that my Dad's getting married in the next two days and I'll be meeting Susan and then once the results are out I am going back to New York. I walk out of the class completely flummoxed.

******

"Casey, please!" Stella shouts out.

"What is wrong with you?" I tell her.

"What's wrong with me, what's wrong with you?" she barks.

"Fine, I'll ask Eric," I reply.

Stella is yet stuck in the rosy picture of me and Eric but I just wish I could tell her the truth. Moreover she wants me to ask Eric for the Prom, it's just so weird and on the other hand I find the Prom boring. I am already so confused and angry with Jason and his note when I see Eric walking towards us. Stella clutches my hand, signalling, I should ask him out. A second later, she excuses herself giving me a naughty smile. He gestures to walk outside the school as the cafeteria is too noisy. On the way, I show him the note,

"I think you should sort things out," he says.

"There's nothing to sort out," I mumble.

"And anyway, I have already made up my mind to move back to New York," I tell him.

"And my Dad's getting married so, I am sure he'll respect my decision," I add.

"You're sounding like a loser here," he taunts.

"And also you are coming with me to the Prom," I inform.

"You can't be serious on this?" he says.

"I am," I reply, smiling.

"Wow," he says, almost blushing.

"Look, don't take me wrong, but I think you should meet Jason, not that I want you to. I mean, anyway you have made up your mind to move back then why keep so much inside yourself. Don't you want to know what exactly he feels for you?" he explains.

"Eric, I understand what you are saying and I would have totally agreed with you, but here, it's Jason. He is so reckless and unpredictable and I... I don't feel he has any mind of telling me the truth," I reply.

"I wouldn't force you after knowing what all he is done to you, the sparkle in your eyes has disappeared completely," he says.

"It's just a matter of time, I'll be fine," I say, smiling my best.

"Thanks for always being there for me," I add.

"It's my pleasure," he says winking and this time around it is different. I guess he has accepted that I can't love him the way he wants me to and that's why maybe, maybe, his eyes smiled back.

I bid him good bye and leave for home with Stella. All the way she keeps blabbering about the dress and the hairstyle and the accessories and on and on whereas my mind is debating against the issue: Should I meet him or should I not? I know Eric was somewhere right and he always is, and also always sweet, but what if things get worse. All this while, I have been silent and trying to heal myself but now, if something goes wrong I wouldn't be able to take it. Stella hugs me tightly before getting out of the car and whispers in my ears,

"Hope you get to kiss him this time."

I smile at her and drive back home. I have learnt this art of escaping my thoughts in the past few days for a while so I guess I will face them tonight.

******

"I was about to call you," Jen says, as I enter the house.

"Whoa, what is going on here?" I say, almost shocked.

The house is turned into a florist shop, there are so many kinds of flowers; roses of almost all colours, lilies, orchids, sunflowers and some more. Jen is walking around the house in her wedding dress and I guess the lady in the black is her Mom.

"Casey, that's my Mom and Mom this is Casey," she introduces us.

I smile at Jen's Mom and feel a little awkward because I've always had one grandma and that's from my father's side.

"Casey, what do you think, is Jennifer looking pretty?" she tries to initiate a conversation.

"Yeah, absolutely, grandma," I reply, smiling.

"Call me Angie, I am too young to be called grandma." She laughs out.

I join in the laughter well, she is really cool. Jen is fidgeting with her wedding dress; well the dress is brilliantly designed. As far as I can notice, it has a lot of fabrics and beads and the one used designing her back is beautiful. The neckline is broad, revealing her shoulders and neck with lacy cap sleeves. The dress has an empire waist with a satin design and the overall silhouette of the dress us more or less like a mermaid, highlighting the lower part of the body with a flowing chapel train sweeping the floor. The veil is beautifully designed using different lace and beads.

"Casey, how do I look?" she questions, playing with the veil.

"Truly a princess, the most beautiful bride ever," I respond, smiling back.

"Quickly remove it before William arrives," Jen's Mom, Angie adds.

"Don't spoil the surprise, Jennifer," I tease her and she rushes back to the room. After a little while, Dad comes home and we have a little chat discussing the wedding and other stuff simultaneously having the dinner.

******

"I don't know what to choose," I wonder to myself. A part of me says that I should meet Jason and the cold and distant part doesn't want me to. I open the note that he had given me and brush my fingers on his handwriting. I can't live with the burden of all these questions all my life. No matter how far I run away, but these questions will always keep haunting me. I need to go, see him for this one last time and sort things out forever. Maybe, just then I'll get some peace of mind. At least I wouldn't regret losing this chance to clear things between us. I do not want to take all these bitter memories back, I want them buried here. All I will take is his emerald green view in my not so sparkly eyes, his warm smile on my lips and I am going to steal a very tiny piece of him; his heart, keeping it secured in mine. I close my eyes, holding his note close to my chest.

I'll always be aching for your love, although you have almost destroyed me; killed me, but I didn't die, even after all this. I'll always be burning in your love. You always looked like everything I wanted; everything I needed, but then you suddenly turned to something I hated. A part of me hates you, a very tiny piece of my body; my mind but the rest is still hopelessly and irrevocably in love with you. I wonder why we have torn apart when my every body part just ... just aches to be with you. I want to be the dream you dream, I want to be the air you breathe in, I want to be the one who increases you heartbeats, I want to be the smile on your lips, I want my soul to be tangled in yours until you break me free.

Chapter 9

"Which one do you think?" Dad questions me for the 5th time, holding a black tuxedo and a dark greyish suit in his hand. I don't know what's wrong with him, today.

"I'll still choose the black one," I reply, again.

"Both are black!" He shouts a little.

"No. The one in your left hand is dark greyish!" I argue. All men are colour blind; hence proved.

"Okay," he says, making a puppy face.

"What?" I bark.

"Nothing." He sighs.

"Dad, it's your wedding; do what you want and wear what you want to. You are the Groom." I explain.

"Yeah, why am I even asking you what to wear in the first place? Your fashion sense is way too out dated," he mocks

"Come again, I didn't hear you," I say, making a deadpan face.

"I am just saying I am going to wear the tuxedo you suggested," he replies.

"Really, well a lot of people tell me, I have an outdated fashion sense," I mock

"What? Who told you?" He says in a dramatic way.

"A man in his mid-forties, who doesn't get the difference between black and grey," I reply hiding my smile.

"Hey, now that is really rude. Mid-forties, c'mon I look at least thirty-five?" He bargains.

"Thirty-five, no way, you look like you have just graduated." I reply and both of us start laughing.

A few seconds later, his cell phone rings and he walks out of my room answering the call. I mentally imagine him wearing the tuxedo and also the suit, "Tuxedo is the best!" I mumble to myself.

"Case, just make sure all your important stuff is locked properly, they are coming!" He almost screams.

"Ohh No." I sigh.

My Dad's cousin sister's twins, they are like cyclones! The last time they were here half of my stuff was misplaced and then I found it in the garage. They are like a real burden. The guests are on their way, maybe in the next three or four hours this house would be turned into a circus. Thank God, that this wedding is a close affair or else I would have gone crazy by now. These two days are undoubtedly going to be C.R.A.Z.Y. The only good thing about the wedding is it keeps me busy and alive and away from those heart breaking thoughts.

******

We have just finished the lunch and I've barely eaten anything because I am too much worked up. My mind is a big chaos and I have to sort things out before everyone arrives, especially before Nick and Neil. So, while Dad is in talks with the Minister, I decide to make a to-do list, just in case I miss anything. I remove the notepad and start jotting down,

Collect Bridesmaid Dresses

Call the Caterer

Meet the florist

Distribute the wedding invites

Confirm the Cake

Check the cars and pre book the cabs

Call Jen

~~*Meet Jason*~~

I immediately cancel the last thing on the list and just then my cell phone rings. I take it out from my pocket and see the name flashing on the screen. I hesitate a little, but then who on earth can resist Jason.

"Hello," I say, sounding all cool.

"Where are you?" he questions. My ears have longed to hear his velvety mysterious voice.

"May I know who this is?" I ask. Well, technically we never exchanged our numbers, but I already have his number for the obvious reasons.

"Your Chemistry project partner, Jason," he replies and I can feel the irritation in his voice.

"Are you coming?" he adds.

"It's difficult," I sigh, but I add something to the to-do list; *definitely meeting Jason!*

"I was wondering if you help me find the information, I'll write for both of us, how about that?" he questions.

WHAT.DID.HE.JUST.SAY! He will write my assignment? Now

I am two hundred percent sure there is something fishy, why is he so curious to see me?

"You sure about it?" I ask him again.

"Absolutely and I'll submit it tomorrow as you would be busy with the wedding preparations," he adds.

WOW! How come my misguided drunken angel suddenly turn into an actual angel?

"Okay, I'll be there in an hour," I say and hang up.

I fold the note neatly and shout out, "Dad?"

"Yeah?" He comes, typing something over the phone.

"I need to go meet someone, for my Chemistry project," I say, hiding my smile.

"Okay but you need to be home before 5." He says, more like an order.

"What time will Aunt Isabel be here?" I ask.

"Maybe around five or something," he says.

"I need to rush and I'll be meeting the florist, collect the dresses and be home ASAP," I explain and rush to my room.

I remove a pair of jeans and a loose off-shoulder T-shirt. I quickly get into them and do not comb my hair because Jason likes me more in my messy hair. I search some information regarding our project, but the bone ash topic seems difficult so, I jot down the links and sites and I also have a few notes back from New York. I keep the notes in my bag, collect the wedding invites and walk out of the house mentally calculating how I am going to manage everything. I get into the car and prepare myself to be normal when around him so that he doesn't come to know how much I have missed him in the past days. I try to figure out the reason behind this sudden urge to meet me as I drive to his house. The moment I get out of the car, I see him already opening the door. Now, that drives me crazy. Has he been waiting for me? If yes, why! I blink my eyes and take a deep breath, pretending to be normal and unaffected by his gesture. He is standing at the door and I in front of him, he smells of mint and as far as my eyes can observe his hair are wet which means he just had his shower. I meet his gaze and then I have a pretty bad time stopping the tears which desperately want to come out of my eyes. He smiles and then I see his eyes rest on my shoulder, a second later, I realize what he is looking at.

"I wear a bra!" I tell him, irritated. I am wearing an off-shoulder T-shirt and my bra strap is clearly visible on one of the shoulders.

"It's the colour," he mumbles.

"I like purple," he adds. I shoot him a deadpan look, bringing him back from his fantasies. Why is he acting so weird, although I like that he at least noticed me.

"I am out of time already, we can talk out your fantasies later," I tell him.

He sheepishly smiles and that smile, makes me fall for him more.

"Aren't you going to let me in?" I say.

"Ohh, sorry," he replies and gestures me to come inside.

I settle myself on the couch and remove the wedding invitation, "Here," I say.

"I'll be there," he replies, smiling.

What is wrong with him? I wonder to myself.

"These are some websites, where you can get the experiment and maybe, this book can be of some help," I say removing it from my bag.

"Okay," he says, looking at the book.

"I am not getting any information related to the bone ash," I explain, searching it in the book.

"Give me a moment," he says and walks in the directions of the stairs, climbing them and finally disappearing somewhere. I look around and see a lot of pictures on the shelf, Jason's childhood pictures, and his parents wedding pictures and a picture where Jason is crying maybe he is a month or two. He undoubtedly looked cute; you cannot resist a smile at him.

"Do you find me cute?" I hear him say, his cool mint breath touching my ears.

"Yes," I say, immediately turning around and distance myself from him.

"Here, check these out," he says, handling me two assignments. I flip the pages and notice that he has already written for both of us and to be precise mine is neater than his. Wow! I being a sincere student can't find the information on bone ash and he has already completed the project, but then why did he call me here?

"But then, why did you call me here?" I question him.

"I wasn't sure about these so, I thought it'd be nice of you if..." he tries to explain.

"Okay, I think these are perfect, especially the section on bone ash," I tell him, reading the assignment.

"Thanks," I say.

"My pleasure," he replies, smiling

My mind is still struggling between what to believe and what not to. I still can't believe that he just wants to see me because he isn't sure about the assignments. Bullshit!

"I guess, I should get going, have a lot of pending work." I sigh.

"Casey," he says and stops.

"What?" I ask him.

"Just stay for a while, please?" he insists.

"Why?" I almost shout, irritated.

"Are you not happy to see me?" he asks and that very moment, I see something change in his eyes.

"I am," I reply, not looking at him and simultaneously pack my bag.

"Well, it doesn't seem like you are?" he adds, and helps me put the book in my bag.

"Jason, what is wrong with you?" I exclaim. He can't always be so unreasonably cute and hypnotize me into believing and doing things his way.

"Everything," he murmurs.

"Why are you doing this to me?" I shout at him and tears strike down my cheeks.

"I am sorry," he mumbles, coming a little too close to me.

"What are you sorry for?" I ask him in my broken voice.

"Everything," he replies and I can't help but believe him.

"I am sorry," he says again and I read the guilt in his eyes.

"That's okay," I say, wiping away my tears.

"I know how it feels to be around so many people and still feel alone," he adds.

"I know that you have been hurt because of me, but trust me I didn't intend to hurt you ever," he explains.

Why is he bringing up all this now, I don't want any explanations for the things he has done to me. And moreover, I don't want the wedding to be spoiled because of me.

"Jason, it's all right. I am getting late, I should leave now," I say, putting the bag on my shoulder.

"I'll be happy if you and your family come to the wedding," I add.

"I'll be there for you, but my family ... well I don't really know where they are," he says and I see the pain screeching in his eyes. I want to ask more, why is he always alone whenever I come to his house or why I haven't heard him talking about his parents all this time. Never. But, opening this topic might change the circumstances between us when everything is healing or to be precise, everything is getting over.

"And don't forget to submit the assignment," I add, and walk a step ahead.

"Yes Ma'am," he replies and I expect him to smile but he doesn't so I just wave my hand and walk to the door.

"Hey," I hear his voice, just when I am about to close the door.

"What?" I ask.

He rushes to the door and says, "I like purple,"

A second later, both of us are laughing, but this time the sound of his laughter isn't peaceful, instead it seemed more like a howl, a painful howl. I convince myself not to look at him and quickly walk to my car. I get into the car and watch him standing in the doorway. I pull the gear and check the first thing on the to-do list; Collect the bridesmaid dress. I recklessly drive the car to the boutique. I am super irritated because I can't really understand Jason's behaviour. Understanding him is like reading between the lines. I stop in front of the boutique and recheck the name; Sapphire, where Jen had ordered our bridesmaid dresses, she had already collected everyone else's just mine and Susan's are left. I mentally prepare myself to try the dresses twice and walk in the boutique.

"Your dresses are absolutely ready," the attendant says when I hand over the receipt to her. She hands me the dresses and I am glad that the boutique is empty.

"Turn left; the changing room is right there," she adds.

"Thanks," I say, smiling and she gets busy filing her nails, chewing a green chewing gum.

I follow the directions pulling my hair into a bun and remove mine from the cover well, the dress is indeed beautiful. I remove Susan's dress, but surprisingly the colour is different. Mine is purple whereas hers is red, usually the bridesmaid wear same colours. I fail to understand the reason behind the colour being different so, instead I try it on. It is a stunning strapless gown, layers of chiffon flow down highlighting the curves of my body. The sweet heart neck is pleated all over until my waistband and reveals a tiny part of my cleavage. I immediately pull my hair down, feeling shy. I try out Susan's dress and I can tell that it is going to fit her perfectly, the dress is a little shorter for my height and a bit loose but it is perfect for Susan. I get into my usual clothes and call Jen to inform her about the dress,

"Where are you?" she says, receiving the call.

"I am at the boutique," I reply.

"Great! So, did you like the dress, does it fit you properl...?" she keeps blabbering.

"Jen," I interrupt her.

"Sorry, I am just a little thrilled with the wedding," she explains.

"The dress is beautiful and it fits perfect, but the colour..."

"You don't like the colour?" she questions.

"No, I absolutely love it but why is it that Susan's dress is red? I mean why the colours are different?" I ask her.

"Because I like colours so, I want all the bridesmaids to be wearing all the colours I like since I'll be the one in white. And also I'd read in some feng shui book that the after marriage life reflects the colours the bride see during the wedding."

"Feng Shui? Really?" I ask her.

"Honey, I'll call you back in a while," she says and cuts the line.

I pack the dress, laughing a little on Jen's idea about wearing different colours. I walk out of the boutique, remembering the next thing to do. I get into the car and call the caterer confirming whether everything is going good and he informs that he has already talked it out with Dad. I immediately drive to the florist for reminding him about the delivery of the bridesmaid bouquets and other decorations. In the meanwhile Dad informs me that the cars and cabs are already taken care of and I just need to check the status of the cake. The cake seems to be in a good position and now the only thing left to do is to give the invites to Stella, Jessica, Mark and Zac; back in school I was in a hurry and I couldn't invite them then. I am driving back home after finishing all the work when I realize that I've to call Susan. Susan's parents can't make it to the wedding because they have some work issues and Dad has taken care of it.

"Where are you?" I yell, parking the car. The second best thing about the wedding is Susan and I've been dying to tell her everything once she'll be here because she is the only person who will help me out with my feelings.

"I am so sorry; I don't think I'll be able to make it." She sighs.

"What? Why?" I shout a little.

"I missed the flight," she informs.

"So, get another one!" I bark.

"There are no tickets available for the next two days," she explains.

"Fine!" I say and cut the line. I take a deep breath and get out of the car. My life is getting totally out of control and this is just the cherry on the cake. I walk to the house, recollecting in my mind if there is anything I've missed. I sigh and open the door and then I just can't move. The house has indeed turned into a circus. Aunt Rachel and Aunt Megan are discussing something about the perfume and their luggage is a mess, all the clothes are scattered around and Aunt Rachel's daughter, Lucy, is wearing heels and playing with a red colour bra! A little ahead Uncle Patrick and Aunt Elena are kind of making out; I immediately look away and walk ahead. Uncle Victor is busy with his laptop and Aunt Gabriel is talking to someone over the phone. I am about to enter the kitchen when I see Uncle Ben, coming out of the washroom and smiling an awkward smile, I smile back at him. Kitchen is another shock, Dad, Grandma and Aunt Isabel are laughing their ass off and that is enough to explain that they are drunk. Aunt Helen and Uncle John are dancing behind them.

"Dad?" I shout my lungs out to get his attention.

"Casey honey, where have you been?" Grandma, questions, finishing the leftover wine.

"Come join us," Aunt Isabel says, pouring some wine in the glass. Before I reply, they are engrossed in themselves again. Everybody here is having a gala time except me. I walk upstairs, irritated and upset with myself for reasons I not know yet. I open the door and *BANG*

"Surprise!" Susan screams.

"You scared the shit out of me!" I yell, hugging her tightly.

"I missed you so much!" she murmurs in my ears.

"I missed you too!" I reply, tears streaking down my cheeks. I open my eyes and I can't understand for a second what is going around in my room.

"Nick!" I shout loud enough, for the entire house to hear.

These two little brothers just boil my blood. Nick and Neil are having moisturizer bottles, no, one has conditioner and for the reasons only known to them, they are applying it all over the walls.

"What are you doing?" I shout, snatching the bottles away from them.

"There are cracks over the walls..." Nick starts.

"So we thought applying the moisturizer would heal the cracks," Neil finishes.

"Both of you; go down." Susan explains to them and they rush out of the room quickly.

She takes the bottles from my hand and walks me to the bed.

"What's wrong with you?" she questions.

"I am just stressed out," I answer.

"Shut this drama and tell me the truth," she orders.

"This is the truth," I say and pray mentally for this topic to end here.

"Case, look I know there is something terribly wrong, although you are trying to be yourself but the past few days, you seemed lost whenever we interacted," she explains.

"It's just..." I run out of words.

"I want to hear the truth." she demands.

"Your wish is my command," I reply and recline on the bed. Susan lies down beside me and I start to tell her everything, staring at the ceiling. She patiently listens to my roller coaster story and doesn't ask me anything on why I'd let Jason kiss me or why I've been into Jason when I knew he had a girlfriend already. She just listens; that's the best thing about her. I end up telling her about meeting Jason today.

"Wow," she remarks.

I still avoid the eye contact and focus on the ceiling.

"Ms Casey Dalton, you hide things from me and call me your best friend, so not done!" She fakes a drama.

"Susan, I did not hide anything." I clarify, making an eye contact.

"Kissing someone who sounds so mysterious is not hiding anything?" She adds to her drama.

"I did not intend to kiss him!" I shout a little.

"The same way I did not intend to lose my V and still called you that night." she adds.

"Lose your V, seriously?" I ask, making a deadpan face.

"Well, at least I shared my fantasy." she replies and we burst out laughing.

"Casey," she says.

"You don't need to find love. The amount of love that belongs to you, will find a way to you, come what may," she explains.

"I hope the amount of love that belongs to me is not in those little moments when I've felt my heartbeats, but in those day dreams that I've been weaving for ages." I sigh.

I look at her and realize that she hasn't changed a bit. She still sleeps hugging a pillow, snores at regular intervals and dozes off when I've a million questions to ask.

I stare at the wall; parts of it covered under the moisturizer. How can the cracks be filled with a mere moisturizer? What an unreasonable thing to do, but what else can we expect from children? All this while, I've too been a child, expecting something from someone who isn't capable of giving me; expecting love from someone who wouldn't even know what love is. Just like the moisturizer can't fill the cracks, but only hide them for a few days, the same way my broken heart can be manipulated for a while until it's broken again. The cracks on the walls disappear once it's painted all over, but my broken heart can only be mended by the one who is capable enough to love me; the broken me.

Chapter 10

Yesterday was an eventful and exhausting day for almost everyone except the bride and the groom. Although I was relieved that we did not have the bachelorette party as the wedding had been planned on a short notice, but we did have the rehearsal dinner, it was like everyone had gone crazy! We had total eight bridesmaids; Emma, Annie, Julia, Sara, Milly, Susan, Me and the smallest bridesmaid, ever Lucy. I was the maid of honour or the senior or chief bridesmaid. The groomsmen include; Uncle Patrick, Uncle Victor, Uncle Ben, Uncle John and Dad's colleague Uncle Justin and of course Nick and Neil. Jen's family was heart warming; Mr Richard Miles was the bride giver-away. Also Richard's wife, Emily helped me decide the background music and the remaining stuff. Then, there was Jen's Mom, Angie, Uncle Aaron and his wife Nancy, Uncle Henry and his wife Kate and Uncle Paul and his son Kevin, who was almost my age. Emma and Annie were Uncle Aaron and Nancy's daughters. Jen's best friend, Selena, couldn't make it to the wedding for reasons unknown to me, but I was happy that both the families were enjoying together.

We practiced the bridesmaid's walk to the aisle and Lucy was the first one to enter with a basket of loose rose petals and spread all over the walkway. Now, that wasn't my idea, but Emily's, Jen's brother's wife. I was the last in the order or you can say I was the senior bridesmaid or the maid of honour who takes care of the bride and also her belongings until the wedding ends. Lucy, Nick and Neil were a big time pain-in-ass, but somehow we managed to convince them about their part. Once the practice was over, Aunt Isabel and Grandma raised a toast and practiced their speech for the reception. Kevin seemed a little uncomfortable, but Susan helped him at being home. There were also arguments regarding the dinner buffet and trust me it was again circus time. I had a high time pretending to finalize whatever they liked and disliked and suggested to add because Dad had already ordered the caterer and warned me that no matter what, I was not supposed to change anything. I was mentally praying to God that it wouldn't snow or rain tomorrow, Chicago weather is unpredictable. Back in New York it snowed late December and as far as I've heard it's the same here. I just wanted it to be warm and sunny tomorrow. We checked and rechecked all the preparations and everything seemed perfect as of then, but again it's a wedding and weddings are never perfect. Something or the other is either left or forgotten or misplaced you know what I mean? I hoped the wedding goes well, fingers crossed.

******

Wedding Day!

"Wow!" Susan exclaims. I observe her reflection in the mirror and she looks really pretty. The dress fits her so well and the perfectly straightened blonde hair makes her look so elegant and sexy. The pearl earrings and the chain add more to her beauty. I wish Daniel was here, he would have probably proposed to her by now.

"You look so pretty," I tell her, turning around.

"I know, right?" she replies.

The straight hair makes your face look prettier, I wish Daniel could have made it to the wedding," I tell her.

"Yeah so do I, but Casey, you make my jaw drop! You look stunning and that little cleavage of yours... I bet a lot of people will have their eyes popping out," she says.

Well, for the first time in a while when I look at my reflection in the mirror I can't help, but stare back at myself. Aunt Rachel has miraculously turned me into a Barbie doll. The only thing that makes me shy is the dress, it is strapless and Aunt Rachel has curled my hair, making a fancy up-do and leaving strands of hair on my face. It is more like a fancy messed up bun or something. The hair is not an issue but because they are tied up, my shoulders and back are naked and that's making me a little shy. Also, since the dress highlights my bodyline a little cleavage is visible, just a little and Susan keeps mocking me about the same. The diamond earrings and the silver bracelet are the only accessories I wear. Studying myself again; the bare shoulders are really making me a little nervous. Besides this I am also wondering whether Jason would find me pretty or maybe hot but again Lyra too would be at her best today, so let's just hope that I get at least a little attention from Jason. Also, the bigger question is, whether he would be turning up at the wedding? Else all my hard work to look noticeable will be in vain.

Everybody looks their best, Aunt Isabel and Grandma look younger than they really are. The other relatives too manage to look presentable. Dad looks really charming in his black tuxedo and he has this big smile glued on his face. Uncle Patrick and Aunt Elena are talking about their wedding and almost everyone is listening, except Susan and me. Whereas Nick, Neil and Lucy are playing with the rose petals and singing Christmas carols. Christmas reminds me of the Prom and I tell Susan that I am in no mood for it. She doesn't try to convince me this time around and for the first time she has given me a little space on such things. She is anyway staying with me for Christmas because

Dad and Jen are going to Paris. Also, Daniel will join us too and I am sure I'll heal with time and then I won't need things to keep myself busy so that I can get over Jason.

******

11 o'clock, Holy Cross Church,

"Jennifer, you look impeccable just stop walking around, you're ruining your hair." I explain to her for the millionth time.

"Okay." She sighs as usual and sits on the only chair in the room. She is the prettiest bride I've ever seen and also Emily, Richard's wife, looks appealing as she is busy adjusting Jen's veil. Jen has this nude makeup and her eyes look larger than usual, but beautiful. Her hair is half-up and the rest loosely curled perfectly. She is wearing emerald earrings surrounded by diamonds, which belong to Angie and that radiates her face. Unlike Dad she doesn't have any smile glued on her face, but tension and nervousness.

Susan is talking over the phone to Daniel and the rest of the bridesmaids, Emma, Annie, Julia, Sara and Milly are busy clicking pictures. We are in the store room which is converted into the bride's waiting room. All the guests are seated in the main hall and a sweet melody is played in the background. Eric, Stella, Jessica, Mark, Zac all of them turn up, but Lyra and Jason seem nowhere. I am getting restless waiting for him. Eric's parents are warm towards me and his Mother giggles something in Eric's ears that makes him laugh. Dad, on the other hand is completely chilled out in his black tuxedo and looks very very charming. We'd been awake last night, discussing stuff about Mom and he seemed a little upset but after like a three hour conversation I convinced him that Mom would have been proud that he wasn't getting wasted.

"Is it time?" Jen questions me.

"I'll just check but you stay here," I tell her and meet Susan in the doorway.

"Please just don't leave her alone," I say.

She nods and I walk to the main hall. I am about to enter the main hall when I see Stella walking towards me, she gives me a thumbs up which means it is time for the bride to make her entry. I quickly rush back to the room and inform everyone. Jen's Mom puts the veil and then our bride is ready. We, the bridesmaids, hold our bouquets and line up for the entrance. We hear the music change and our little bridesmaid walk forward to the main hall, spreading petals of roses all around the walkway. We calculate the time and Emma walks out of the room followed by Annie, Julia, Sara, Milly, Susan and last, but not the least me. I am very nervous and pray to God that I don't create any mistakes. I hear the music beat change and I start walking towards the main hall. I squeeze the bouquet in my hand, hiding my nervousness and take small but determined steps. I avoid making any direct eye contact and keep looking all around, mostly at Dad. He keeps smiling his brilliant smile and I smile back at him. Everybody's attention is on me, but these two dark emerald eyes make me a lot conscious. I have goose bumps all over me, when my eyes find him in the crowd. It is like a mini heart attack well, at least he turned up. I climb up the stage and stand in my position, yet avoiding direct eye contact. The music changes again and the minister announces,

"Everyone please rise for the entrance of the bride."

Everybody in the main hall stands up, their heads turn to the entrance. A second later, I see Jen and her brother, her best-man or the bride giver-away, Richard walking from a distance. She is a vision in white, trust me everybody's eyes are popped out and my Dad, his mouth is half open. Jen walks through the aisle, her smile so radiant that you can't even blink your eyes.

"We have gathered today, for this very special and sacred occasion. Thank you, all for your presence in the celebration of these two becoming one." The minister says and everybody settles back.

"Who gives this woman to be married to this man?" He questions, looking at Jen's brother, Richard.

"I, her brother, on behalf of my parents," Richard informs and Dad takes Jen's hand, helping her climb on the stage. The bride and groom stand facing each other, I am standing beside Jen and it is interesting to watch Dad nervous and excited, both together.

"It is recorded in Genesis chapter 2 of the Bible, Marriage is sacred; God himself gave the first bride away. God himself performed the first wedding ceremony." He pauses and then continues.

"The lord God said, it is not good for the man to be alone. I will make a helper suitable for him. For this reason the man will leave his father and mother and be united to his wife and the two become one flesh." He finishes.

I shift my attention from my Dad and Mum, now officially, and search for Jason in the crowd. It takes me a glance to find him; he is looking in my direction and that makes me smile wider. The smile is not because he too is looking at me, but for the things I've been doing since morning to look this perfect.

"William Dalton and Jennifer Miles, realizing the sacredness of this relationship who now make with one another," I hear the Minister.

"Having made this legal and public declaration would you please signify the desire to enter into the bond of marriage by joining hands." The minister adds.

I take Jen's bouquet from her hand as they both hold each other's hands.

"William, please repeat after me," the Minister says.

"I, William Dalton, take you, Jennifer Miles to be my wife, to have and to hold from this day forward, for better and for worse, for richer, for poorer, in sickness and in health, to love and to cherish, till death do us apart." I see Dad repeating the words, looking into Jen's eyes taking the vows clearly and loud enough to echo the entire church. I can feel the happiness in his voice.

"Jennifer, please repeat after me," the Minister says.

"I, Jennifer Miles, take you, William Dalton to be my husband, to have and to hold from this day forward, for better and for worse, for richer, for poorer, in sickness and in health, to love and to cherish, till death do us apart." Jen repeats the vows looking back into Dad's eyes, blushing at the same time.

"Do you, William Dalton take Jennifer Miles to be your lawfully wedded wife?" The Minister questions Dad.

"I do." He answers.

"Do you, Jennifer Miles take William Dalton to be your lawfully wedded husband?" The Minister questions Jen.

"I do." She replies.

Everybody claps and Uncle Patrick whistles once, but all my attention is either on Mum and Dad or on my Greek God.

"Now, what do you have as a token of your love?" The Minister questions Dad.

Richard hands over the rings — or the token of love — that are to be exchanged to one of the groomsmen.

"The ring is the time honoured symbol of the marriage ceremony and the marriage relationship shared between two souls. The purity of gold speaks the purity of love between Jennifer and

William. The ring is an unending circle, a picture of permanence of the marriage relationship." He completes, giving the rings to both of them. They make each other wear the ring, in their very own ring finger. Another round of applause and the entire church echoes with the noise of claps.

"Now, if you both would repeat these words after me," the Minister interferes.

"With this ring, I pledge my life and love to you, as your companion and friend. I will help you to become the person God intends you to be. I will be honest, trustworthy and faithful so long as we both shall live." Mum and Dad complete this additional vow.

"And now Mr William Dalton, you may kiss the bride!" He announces with a smile and soon after the announcement, I see them becoming one as they kiss.

"I pronounce you husband and wife, ladies and gentlemen, Mr and Mrs Dalton!" He adds, ending the marriage ceremony. They turn towards me, smiling. I love you both; I move my lips silently and see their smiles getting wider. I stand there, watching them walking to the table to sign the legal documents and then I shift my gaze to Jason. He is playing around with Nick and Neil. I look away and then back at him wondering what it would be like to be married to him. I rest my eyes on the rose bouquet, imagining the whole scenario. I'll be the one in white and he'll be the one waiting for me at the aisle. I'll be so nervous and would still manage to look average in front of my breathtakingly impeccable Greek God. How we would hold our hands while the Minister reads from the Bible, I am sure he wouldn't be listening to any of that and instead keep playing with my fingers and how I would forget the vows or speak the wrong words getting all nervous in his presence and...

"Casey, Case?" I hear Susan's voice and my daydream is scattered just the like the dew drops on the rose petals.

"I'll be back in a moment," I tell her and hand her over Jen's bouquet.

I quickly walk to the store room, my heart heavy with the pain trying to make its exit through my eyes. I stand facing the window, watching the view ahead. Tears escape my eyes and I know the thing that I keep searching outside the window is actually in the main hall. I feel someone behind me, it must be Susan, I wonder. I turn around, hugging her tightly and bury myself into her, but the moment our bodies' touch each other I realize it isn't her, it is him. I immediately pull myself away from him, completely embarrassed.

"What's wrong?" He questions, as soon as we are apart.

"Nothing," I reply, looking at the floor, tears filling in my eyes all set to escape.

"Casey," he says, cupping my face in his hand. He lifts up my chin and I have no other option but to look into his eyes. He wipes the tears away and whispers,

"I never knew, even dinosaurs can cry," he says mimicking like a child. I could have answered but I am not sure what is making me cry and that makes me cry even more.

"Sweetheart, what's wrong?" he questions, yet again and I can see him getting a little tensed.

"I don't know," I mumble, jerking his hands away and turning back to the window.

I feel his breath around my shoulder. A second later, I feel something on my neck with his hands touching my upper back. I see a pendant resting on my neck; it is a round circle in silver and the word 'Love' is embossed on it with a tiny diamond beside 'e'. I turn back to him with a big question mark on my face.

"A little gift for the prettiest bridesmaid I've ever seen," he winks.

The same ridiculous smile comes back on my face charmed with the gesture, but a moment later I am back to my unreasonable self.

"No, I can't take this," I say, trying to open the chain.

"Well, why not?" he questions, making a puppy face.

"Please just..." I run out of words and place the pendant-chain in his palm.

He stares at the pendant and murmurs, "Ms Casey Dalton, I was wondering would you like to accompany your misguided drunken angel to the Prom Night?"

As soon as he completes the sentence and meets my eyes I am frozen in that moment. I can hear my heart throbbing in my chest. I part apart my lips to speak something but I am awestruck. I just stare at him, trying to recollect myself and frame a sentence, but all that escapes my lips is just air. He doesn't blink his eyes and I don't blink mine, either. He brings himself close to me, so close that I can breathe his perfume. All this while, his eyes are screaming for the answer I've wanted to say, but I am just lost in him. He smiles and I smile back automatically, a second later, our smiles meet each other. His soft cold fingers touch my arms and then my shoulder, finally resting on my cheek while the other play along my back, he runs his fingers around my bare back, pulling me towards himself and fixing the chain again in my neck. I taste his warm lips, my hands on his shoulders, never wanting to let him go.

"I'll take this as a yes," he whispers, breathing heavily. I feel his heartbeats on my palm as I rest it on his chest, calming my thirsty soul. His lips touch my forehead soon after he completes the sentence and he breaks my embrace, walking out of the room. I stand there, feeling all loved and wanted.

******

Once the minister declares them as husband and wife, everybody is busy clicking pictures whereas I am stunned. I click a few pictures with Dad and Mum, but my mind is still tangled in that very moment of bliss. I am looking around for Jason but he is nowhere? Can you believe that? The guy who just asked me out for Prom and just ... just kissed me is nowhere? What is he like, a ghost? Sometimes, I think he just doesn't exist and all this is just my imagination! After clicking the pictures we move upstairs to the reception hall. The hall is beautifully decorated with orchids and lilies, brightly lit. The tables and the chairs are properly situated with an orchid bouquet on each of them. Everybody gets settled and then it is time for the cake cutting ceremony. It is a four layer white chocolate cake with the usual groom and bride on the topmost layer, it is decorated with creamy designs and artificial flowers encircled the entire cake with a 'just married' tag on it. Soon after that the lunch starts, the buffet menu has a lot of stations; Drinks Station, BBQ Station, Miniature Station, Italian and Asian and rest of them I am not able to read. The food course includes potato dough and spring rolls, roasted chicken thighs with bacon and parsley, vegetable white and brown rice, sweet and sour chicken, burgers, roasted Italian potatoes, spaghetti, pasta with Italian sausage and bell pepper, grilled vegetable medley, etcetera. The drinks station has iced tea, lemonade, fruit punch and champagne while the dessert station has cherry pie and hot fudge sundae. I eat some pasta, chicken with the vegetable rice and fruit punch. Susan,

Stella, Eric, Jessica, Mark and Zac have made a little pack of their own and they are having a good time together. On the other end their parents are accompanied by Aunt Elena and Uncle Patrick. Once I am done, I help everyone at the wedding and make sure about whatever they need. Almost everybody make two trips to the buffet and when everybody seems over with the lunch we start the toast. Since Richard is the best man, we decide it will be a great start hearing from the bride's brother.

Ladies and Gentlemen,

I've been looking forward to this moment for a long time now and it feels great to see everyone enjoying the wedding today. Jennifer is a truly awesome creature I've shared my life with, she is so irritating and at the same time so adorable. I remember a lot of my childhood was spent running behind her and fighting with each other, but now if I look behind I'd proudly say that I am proud to be the brother of Jennifer Miles. And this is the first time I've been able to speak for five minutes in Jennifer's presence without being interrupted. I wish the happy couple well and toast their future happiness. Ladies and gentlemen, to the bride and groom!

Aunt Isabel and Grandma have their short toast speech and then everybody is in themselves as the background music starts. So, after everyone is done with the toast, the only ceremony left is tossing the bouquet. All the bridesmaids are positioned to catch the bouquet anyhow even Susan and Stella! Can you imagine? I stand a little away from them; wedding is surely not in my bucket list as of now. I watch Mum throw her bouquet in the air and all the bridesmaids try hard to catch it. Susan lands up with the bouquet and she is screaming her heart out with happiness. I wonder what it would be to marry someone you love.

"Honey," Mum comes walking to me, after the bouquet ceremony. I smile at her, hiding the pain in my heart.

."This one's for you," she says, pulling out a red rose.

"Why?" I ask her.

"I removed it from my bouquet, since you are too young for marriage so..." She pauses and I laugh a little as she sounds like a real mother.

"I thought this red rose might bring the love that is meant for you. It's a good omen." She completes.

"Thanks, Mum," I reply, taking it from her.

"Mum seriously?" She laughs it off.

"Jen is perfect!" she adds.

"Okay, thanks Jen," I say and we both hug each other. I have a little moisture in my eyes, when we hug each other. Soon after we wrap up the wedding and Mum, I mean Jen and Dad leave for Paris, yet confirming if I have changed my mind and want to join them. I explain to them that I am a grown up now and even Susan is staying back so there is no need to worry. Well, I could have given it a thought but after Jason asked me out even thinking about Paris is a sin to me. We bid them farewell and start moving back home after biding Jen's family a warm goodbye.

Marriage is a union of two hearts; two souls, a husband and a wife It is an adventure that makes you both; happy and sad for the rest of your life.

BOOK JASON

I drive back home, finally asking her out for the Prom, but on the way I see David and Lyra, sitting at the coffee shop. I immediately park my car and hurriedly walk to them. The moment I reach their table, David excuses himself, David is Lyra's ex-boyfriend and she'd promised me that she will never ever talk to him again. I bring her out, away where we can calmly talk it out, and wait for a few seconds for some justification, but she keeps mum.

"What's going on?" I ask her and wait for her to reply.

"Lyra, I am asking you God damned, why aren't you answering my question? What were you doing with him?" I ask again.

"Believe me, I was just trying..." She runs out of words.

"It's over!" I shout at her.

"Jason, I swear I haven't cheated on you. I love you," Lyra begs.

"Then what is all this? Huh? What is he doing here and why did he excused himself as soon as he saw me?" I shout.

"No! It is all a misunderstanding, he just bumped into me. Please, believe me!" She cries.

"It's over, Lyra," I declare and get into the car. Pulling the gear I dial Casey's number and disconnect it immediately.

"I am so sorry, Lyra," I murmur to myself out of guilt, but I can't afford to lose Casey, I can't let her slip out of my hands. The memory is still fresh in my mind, when she'd bumped into me. She was furiously nagging about how messy she was and her eyebrows arching the worry on her forehead while her soft fragile hands collected the books. I had been hearing, since morning among the boys about this newbie; Casey Dalton. She was effortlessly beautiful and I am sure that she is unaware about the fact that when her tiny dark pink lips keep moving around continuously, you can't help yourself, but just stare at them. Her black hair fell across her radiant face and she brushed them away immediately, a little irritated. She finally looked up to me, when she realized that someone was there to help her. Her big black eyes were alluring, filled with innocence and a little touch of mischief. People often say, eyes are windows to the soul and if that were true, her soul sparkled in her eyes. Her eyes also conveyed to me that she was highly embarrassed about this bumping-into-me-out-of-nowhere-moment, although I considered that a moment of pure bliss. I watch myself in her eyes as she recollected herself. Well, it was obvious she was charmed by me but somewhere I was enchanted by her too; her simplicity and the innocent awkwardness she carried around herself. The entire Chemistry class, she was so conscious, I heard her heart beating. It was like a drum, so loud. And when I'd opened her hair, just to see how she'd react, she was frozen for a second.

I park the car and open the door, my mind consumed with her, entirely. My cell phone is flooded with Lyra's calls and messages. I turn it off and walk to my room, removing a bottle of water from the refrigerator. I free myself from the suit, and lay on the bed in my spongebob-squarepants boxers. Thank God, Lyra didn't turn up at the wedding today or else the entire breakup plan would have failed! Also, I wouldn't have had my moment with Casey if she would have been around. I just can't get the wedding scenario out of mind, especially Casey. I replay the wedding closing my eyes. As the music changed, I watched the bridesmaids one by one making the entrance to the main hall, anxiously waiting for Casey. I was losing all my patience to be precise; I am an impatient person and waiting for her made me restless. Finally, she entered and that very moment my heart stopped beating. She was like a dream. I bet none of us could take our eyes off her, at least I couldn't. The purple dress flowed around her hourglass figure, tracing her body perfectly. Her hair was pulled backward into a messy hairdo, revealing her snow white shoulders and her back. The dark pink lips were curved into a smile, her cheeks flushing red it was obvious she was nervous. As she walked through the aisle, carefully avoiding eye contact with anybody in particular I saw her hands clenching the red bouquet a little too much. Now, that made me scare a little, I thought she might hurt her fragile hands. Finally, her gaze met mine for a brief second and I saw my entire world captured in them; they sparkled that very moment. She looked timeless, the day she'd bumped into me and this present day she hadn't changed a bit; rather I'd say, every time I look at her she seems to be the same, just more beautiful and irresistible. And on top of all this, she wore purple, now was that because I told her that I like that colour or was it a coincidence?

Her face keeps flashing in front of my eyes, I am happy that I'd finally asked her out for the Prom. She was so startled when I'd asked her, her eyes kept screaming the word YES! I smile remembering the kiss we'd shared. I love the way her breathing changes as soon as I touch her. Her warm breath on my needing lips as they entangle into each other. I was so lost in that kiss, all I remember is I was trying to pull her towards myself and even when the distance disappeared she still didn't feel close enough. My fingers playfully lingered around her bare back, making her kiss me more passionately. I'd opened my eyes for a second, just to make sure that she was right there, with me, in my arms, kissing me like I've never been kissed before; my own little paradise. Her soft hands were around my shoulders embracing me completely and then resting over my chest. I am sure she would have felt my heartbeats as her palm rested over my heart; my heart that belongs to her, now. I was breathless at the end of the kiss, leaving a part of me on her lips as I walked away, not that I wanted to, but I didn't want to confess my feelings at her Dad's wedding! That would be so awkward and most importantly I want it to be the best moment of Casey's life after all that I've done to her.

Suddenly I start to visualize our wedding; mine and Casey's. I'll be standing at the altar waiting for her and she'll walk in wearing the white dress, clenching the bouquet yet again. And then when the Minister will tell us to hold our hands, but instead I'll keep playing with her fingers and maybe we would add our own vows. The best part will be the kiss, she'll be all nervous, but I'll purposely kiss her intensely. I just hope her heartbeats wouldn't echo in the church then. Later, at night she would argue with me naked about how I kept making her nervous at the wedding and I'll let her win, I'll always let her win when she fights naked, who wouldn't? I dream about our lives a few years down the line with our kids; a boy and a girl and I imagine how we would fight on what to name them and how I'll be playing in the lawn with them and she'll be the perfect mother and a wife and I'll try my best to keep her happy. Then, my thoughts divert to how I should propose to her for the wedding, I know this is too early, but I don't plan to let her go away until she wants to. I keep thinking about the proposal, should do the typical kneel down one or should I plan a date or should I just...

******

I open my eyes and realize I slept dreaming about her, our wedding. I switch my cell phone on, getting out of the bed and walk downstairs to the kitchen. I check the cell phone hoping that Casey may have texted me, but all the messages are from Lyra. I walk back and sit on the couch, sipping the coffee from the mug, but only to spit it out.

"Yuck!" I mutter angrily, the coffee tastes too bitter. A second later, my phone flashes Lyra calling. I am already feeling guilty on breaking up with her for something that she hasn't even done, but I am helpless.

"Jason, please don't leave me." She starts as soon as I answer her call.

"Lyra, look it's just not worth it," I reply.

"Just listen to me, please," she requests. I disconnect the line and think of some logical reason to get rid of her completely. I mean why can't she just understand and leave me alone. She keeps calling me on a loop and I don't receive any of them but when the calls don't stop I finally answer one of them.

"Lyra just let me be." I bark.

"For one last time Jason, are you going to come back to me?" she asks her voice strong like iron.

"No, never," I reply, immediately.

"Fine, go fuck yourself and you know what? I actually did cheat on you, but not with David. I've been dating Austin and Lucas for like five months now, so you can't dump me, but I dump you!" She screams her lungs out. So, the Austin part was indeed true, I wonder to myself.

"What do you think; I didn't know about you and Austin? Just for your kind information I always knew that you both made out in the locker room and also, I have a video!" I bark louder, I am angry.

"What?" She says from the other end.

"Yes and you bug me one more time, I swear I am gonna make it go viral!" I scream.

"What?" Her voice is breaking.

"So go fuck yourself!" I shout and cut the line.

Once the conversation ends, there is a big grin on my face. I am relieved, finally Lyra is out of my world and on top of that now she'll be scared about the video thing that I'd never made. I sip the coffee from my mug and spit it out yet again, finding myself smiling. Her words kept ringing in my ears, "You're a dinosaur." That entire night she acted like a drama queen; a cute drama queen. I remember every detail about that night, how she was flirting around with Eric, but I know her too well and also that she was trying to make me jealous. Talking was okay, but when she'd rested her head on Eric's shoulder I so hated that moment. Eric is a really really nice guy, but Casey needs someone like me or rather I need someone like her. I dial her number out of curiosity.

"Mmm..." she mumbles receiving the call.

"Case?" I call her out, a little confused.

"Mmmm," she mumbles again.

"Casey!" I shout a little, failing to understand what is going on.

"Yeah," I finally hear her speak, in her sleepy voice. It is then I realize that the wedding would have tired her out and she must be sleeping.

"Hi, this is Jason," I speak whatever comes to my mind and I know I sound lame.

"I recognize your voice," she replies, her voice soothing my ears.

"You do?" I ask her feeling happy that she remembers me even when she's asleep.

"Jason... I ... am rea...llly sleep...y," she completes the sentence with a lot of pauses, she sure is sleepy, but her voice kind of turned me on.

"So Casey," I stop in between trying to figure out what should I say.

"Yes Jason," she whispers. I feel her breath through the cell phone well; I didn't know my voice too changes her breathing.

"Uhh, nothing you should sleep my alluring knight in shining armour, goodnight," I tell her, getting out of words.

"You just called me in the middle of the night to say good night?" she questions from the other side.

"I guess so," I reply, checking the time. She is really sleepy, because eight o'clock seems middle of night to her.

"Good night," she whispers and cuts the line. Well, I didn't want to hang up although we talked nothing sensible, but I'd do anything to listen to those sleepy whispers. I wonder what she'd be dreaming of, would it be me? Or is she awake this very moment and blushing under the blanket that is all over her? I so wish I could that blanket that gets to touch her skin; her soul. Also, I'd be the only boyfriend on earth who is so happy about the break up. I did felt guilty at first, but when your own ex-girlfriend confesses that she'd been cheating on you all this time, at a moment when all you want is to break up, you can't help but smile like an idiot! This is just like a cherry on the cake.

I switch on the T.V. ordering a barbeque chicken pizza and go back to the couch. I keep switching the channels back and forth out of boredom. I glance at the cell phone, lying on the couch and expect it to flash Mom calling or either Dad, but maybe I am wishing too much. All my life I have been abandoned by my loved ones, always. Mom and Dad are so busy pursuing their dreams that they've almost forgotten me. I am not saying that they do not love me, but just sending me money and getting me whatever I want is not enough. There are times when I miss them and I know that even they do, just a little less than me. All of the things I've loved or the people I love have been taken away from me in some or the other way. I have lost my grandpa and my favourite football and my parents and I couldn't risk Casey. I can't afford to lose her, that's the only reason I've been waiting and hurting her in a way. I fear losing her, like everyone, like everything that's been taken away from me.

I flip the channel and the movie *X-men* is tuned on, my lips are curled into a smile, immediately. The memory of the drunken night, not mine, but hers flashes across my eyes. She was right here, beside me on this couch and we were exchanging the dialogues until we both closed our eyes as she fell asleep in my arms. I felt something soft brushing against my lips, I recognize the touch of her lips; Casey had kissed me, ON MY LIPS! That night when I looked at her, I'd seen a rose bud blooming in my arms. She cuddled into me like a child cuddles in the blanket. Although her innocence was incommensurable with that of the child, who slept cuddled in that very blanket. She looked like Love wrapped around cupid's arrow; pure and real. Her hands folded and her fingers curled into a fist, grasping my shirt softly underneath. The dark pink lips met each other, the lower one inverted a little on the inside. I gently touched her chin, bringing it out. Her heartbeats got steady and slowed down at once, I tried matching mine with hers but mine remained steady; always. I looked at those eyes, perfectly shut and tried to count her long black eyelashes. In a matter of time, my eyes were heavy. I held her in my arms, just encircling her a little too close to myself and closed my eyes. That night something changed in me; inside me. Maybe it was love. I hoped it was love because nothing since my existence had ever made me feel what that moment did; it stopped the noise in my mind. I was caught up in that moment unable and unwilling to escape.

The doorbell rings bringing me out of my paradise. I walk to the door, removing some money from my wallet. I place the pizza on the couch, bringing a chilled beer bottle from the kitchen and settle on the couch. I flip the channels, eating the pizza, ending up watching a football game. The game is between Netherlands and Costa Rica, it has been 20 minutes already and none of the team succeeds to make a goal. I have two slices of pizza and I am done, my appetite has shrunk terribly in these years. I drink the beer, watching the game. The Costa Rica team clearly has no chance winning against Netherlands not because it's my favourite team but because their coordination is just superb. Netherlands is trying it's best to score a goal but the only good thing about Costa Rica is their goal keeper. The goal keeper seems to be the only one who plays his ass off, the rest of the players, are just running around and have completely forgotten that they too have to score a goal. An hour has passed and none out of both teams' scores a goal, the game is getting frustrating now! I switch the T.V. off and look at the leftover beer inside the bottle. My heart keeps skipping beats as I recollect the memory, of my first ever kiss. Okay, I've been kissed before, but none calmed my soul quite like her lips did. Who would have thought that a mere bottle of beer could have helped experience my first kiss. Yes, I remember the kiss we exchanged near the church and every detail about that night.

I was drunk that night, but I was in my senses. Mark, the guy who accompanied me that night to the club with his girlfriend, who broke up with him, after she found out he was kissing someone else. We were walking back home when I'd coincidently seen Casey at the church. Mark was drunk and he'd screamed out loud that she was Hot! Later, I walked towards her, but she seemed too scared to even turn around and look at me. I breathed her in and she smelled of strawberries. It was a starry night with a full moon, nonetheless a beautiful one, her snow white face glowed in the darkness as the moonlight scattered all around. Her bloodshot lips quivered a little escaping warm air out and her eyes, innocent and dreamy, twinkled like pearls. I couldn't take my eyes off her. I tried to initiate a conversation with her and she wouldn't believe me no matter how hard I tried to convince her that I wasn't too drunk; so I just gave up. And when she believed that, I was really drunk I behaved like I really was. She kept asking me questions and I answered some of them, so that conversation kept going on and on, the entire night if possible. She kept asking me my address, but I didn't want her to leave me, not then, never. So, I removed a rose from under my jacket which belonged to Mark but I'd do anything to divert her mind. I spoke something terribly cheesy and made her laugh, her voice soothed my ears and before she could ask me some more questions I touched her lips with my finger, sealing them together. I pulled her close to myself, her eyes widened a little and her eyebrows curved on her forehead. I didn't know why but my lips were dying to be on hers, it was like I didn't control myself but she did; her touch. Finally, we were close enough for our lips to meet. That night I tasted bliss and she'd kissed me back like, like she'd never been kissed before; like she'd never been loved before.

I remember how she'd taken me to her house and taken care of me when she barely knew me. We were just one Chemistry class old and also one kiss, that I'd pretended to forget because I was scared that she might not talk to me again and I would never be able to find out what my heart holds for her. There have been times that I've acted unreasonable and she has had every reason to hate me but she just didn't instead she kept surprising me. She has so many sides to herself; sometimes she's so nervous and sometimes so outspoken that you wouldn't know what to reply and sometimes she's funny and sometimes she acts like a dude and sometimes she's too shy. God! She's unpredictable like a magic trick, you never know what's gonna happen next! The only constant thing amongst her sides is that she talks through her eyes; her eyes are a mirror of reflections. She's always there for me, even when I am at my darkest and wouldn't complain about anything. I drink the leftover beer and lie back on the couch, feeling restless.

She is asleep this very moment, I so wish I could be there or she could be here, right beside me or in my arms or over me or anywhere around me. Our legs intertwined together, sharing a single blanket. Her soft skin touching mine, her hands stroking my hair as her eyes convey her love to me. I gently trace my lips against hers, conveying my love back. My heart has already planned a lot of things for just us; her and me, alone, together. I want her to sit on my kitchen counter wearing my shirt; just my shirt and talk about random stuff as I make her a hot chocolate or relax in the bath tub and tell her how she makes me happy. I want her to kiss me when I am in the middle of saying something or light me up when I am at my darkest. I want to smell her hair, hold her hand and buy her roses and surprise-hug her from behind when she's not expecting me to. I want her to strip tease for me when I am not paying attention and when she finally has all of me; I want her to get mad at me until I kiss the heaven out of her. I'll let her shave my face and I'll go places with her and get her drunk, spoil her and do the craziest shit ever. I want to slow dance with her under the shower and I'll let her wear my clothes not because she wants to or she looks adorable in them but because it kind of turns me on. I want to wake up in love and sleep making love; with her.

I am in love with her and I want her just the way she is. She is full with hopes and desires and I am a broken soul, loving her with my damaged heart. I am in love with all her sides and I can't tell you which one out of them all is my favourite. But all I know is that she has always loved me consistently even when I was undeserving. I was torn apart, but since the day we met, she has stitched me back, carving her name on my heart. And now even if I want to forget her, my heart never will. In so little time she's occupied my body and soul that I feel incomplete without her; my days just wouldn't end if I don't think of her and my nights are empty if I don't dream of her. Everything seems empty without her now, it's like when she is around me my world seems to be a beautiful place and the moment she's gone my world starts to fall apart. She owns me now and I am privileged to love her right back for eternity.

Chapter 11

"Bye, honey. Take care of yourself." Aunt Isabel kisses me good bye.

"Yeah, you too," I reply, smiling.

After Jen and Dad leave for Paris, we come back home and then everybody starts leaving. Aunt Isabel and Grandma stay back until everyone leaves, since they know I am tired and also that I have problems handling Nick and Neil. Thank God! They behaved at the wedding and everything went perfect. Susan is staying back and she has already informed Daniel to come over for celebrating Christmas. I am tired and happy and confused, confused because I couldn't understand why Jason asked me to the Prom.

"Jennifer is a wonderful woman and I am sure she'll be a great mother," Grandma says, hugging me.

"She sure is," I reply. They leave after making sure that Susan and I will be fine all alone.

******

"Why are you smiling so much?" Susan questions me, as we head upstairs.

"Am I?" I question confused.

"Yes and I am sure it's not because the wedding went off well," she adds.

I do not reply and try to get out of the dress which seems really difficult,

"What? Aren't you going to tell me?" She shouts.

"Help me get out of this dress first!" I shout back. I'll do whatever she says to get out of this dress, my boobs are hurting now. Finally, Susan gets the dress off my body and I can comfortably breathe in. I remove a loose T-shirt from the closet mentally deciding to wear a bra or not, I conclude with the latter and get into the Tee.

"Casey!" Susan barks.

"Relax!" I reply.

"Will you just tell me right now like this very momen..."

Before she completes, I interrupt, "I just had the best prom-posal ever!"

"What?" she says all confused.

"Yes, Jason wants to take me to the Prom ... with him ... and he ... just asked me out ... at the wedding ... and..." I explain her with deliberate pauses.

"Holy Shit!" she shouts.

"And..." I pause, untangling my hair.

"And, what?!" she asks, curiously.

"He ... kissed ... me again and also gifted me this," I tell her, showing the chain on my neck. She looks all startled at first and keeps gaping at the chain.

"THIS.IS.SO.FUCKING.AWESOME!" She screams, hugging me.

"I know," I reply, blushing. Somewhere in my mind there are a lot of questions going unanswered, but I am too tired to let them out, this very moment.

She changes her clothes and informs me that Daniel will come over in the morning. Jason asking me for the Prom seems still fishy somewhere because I can't really accept it. Anyway, I am exhausted so I lock the house properly, drink some milk and come back to the room. Susan is talking to Daniel over the phone and I calmly wait until she gets over with it. Once she gets off the phone, we burry ourselves into the blanket the way we always did and keep talking whatever come to our minds. She keeps talking about Daniel and how much she misses me and I tell her that I still can't believe that Jason just asked me out. Also, I give the details about our kiss and how he was worried when I wasn't answering him about what made me cry. I don't remember how and when we slept and who slept first but I wake up with my phone buzzing in the middle of the night. My eyes are too heavy to check the name on the screen so I press the button.

"Mmm..." I say, receiving the call.

"Case?" Someone says, from the other end and I try to recognize the voice.

"Mmmm," I mumble back.

"Casey!" He shouts a little and I remember it's Jason.

"Yeah," I reply, trying hard to open my eyes and understand why he is calling me in the middle of the night.

"Hi, this is Jason," he adds, after a moment.

"I recognize your voice," I reply, half asleep.

"You do?" he questions.

"Jason... I ... am rea...llly sleep...y." I try to speak, without passing out.

"So Casey," he starts to speak something but then stops.

"Yes Jason," I whisper back, assuring him that I am up.

"Uhh, nothing you should sleep my alluring knight in shining armour, goodnight," he says.

"You just called me in the middle of the night to say good night?" I question him, confused.

"I guess so," he replies.

"Good night," I respond and cut the line because it is really difficult to be awake. A second later, I finally open my eyes and the room is dark, no night lamp, nothing. It doesn't seem like a good idea to check the time in my phone because my eyes will really hurt and also, I am too lazy to remove my hand from the blanket. I mentally calculate the time, closing my eyes. The wedding was over around 6:00 p.m. and by the time everybody left it was around quarter to seven and then Susan and I went off to sleep. It may be around 2:00 a.m. or something, I conclude. I think about the rose that Jen gave me at the wedding. She told me that it's going to bring the love that is meant for me; well, didn't the rose thing worked too fast? I am too sleepy to understand whether it really is because of the rose or something else. Jason could anyway change his decision, there's still a day and a half left for the Prom. I close my eyes and it doesn't take me a moment to go back to sleep.

******

I come out of the sleep, checking the time in the clock; 1:00 p.m. I look around for Susan but she is nowhere in the room so I snuggle a little into the blanket. My body aches so; I stretch a little and close my eyes again. A second later, I rush out of the room shouting,

"SUSAN!"

"SUSAN, why didn't you..." I shut my mouth as I see Daniel, sitting beside Susan on the couch. It is so embarrassing!

"What?" she questions me weirdly.

"Nothing," I reply, walking back to my room. I keep cursing myself for the next five minutes.

"I am sure I've had more embarrassing moments in my life," I mumble to myself. I am brushing my teeth when I hear Susan's voice in my room,

"Casey?" she shouts a little.

I come out of the wash room brushing my teeth and looking around to see if Daniel too has followed her.

"What's wrong with you?" she questions.

I just wave my hand in the air, trying to speak something, but I can't.

"Why were you shouting a few minutes back?" she adds. I finally rinse my mouth and say,

"I just realized that I'm going to the Prom, with Jason!"

"Huh?" she questions again.

"Nothing, I need to go meet Daniel," I say and we walk out of the room. I study her expression and she seems clueless about the conversation that had taken place a few seconds back.

"Daniel!" I call him out smiling.

"Congratulations, on your Dad's wedding," he says, smiling. Although he is my best friend's boyfriend yet we don't share a comfort level and it's not him but me, I always keep acting weird and awkward.

"Thanks, does Susan bug you too much?" I question him, teasing Susan a little.

"Nah, but I guess she has half a mind to convert me into a girl, she keeps blabbering about the lasted brands and sometimes even lingerie," he answers, laughing.

"Lingerie?!" I question, looking towards Susan.

"What? It's good to discuss, I come to know the colour he likes." Susan replies.

"Whatever, you guys are the craziest creatures in love on earth." I say and walk to the kitchen. Well, of course they are not the craziest people in love because I remember Jason telling me that he liked my purple colour bra, not exactly my bra but the strap or maybe just the colour purple! I blankly smile removing some corn flakes in the bowl, when Susan arrives.

"Why are you acting all weird?" she questions.

"Am I?" I ask her not knowing what to answer, pouring some milk from the milk-carton.

"Yes, you are!" she snaps.

"Forget that, what are you doing here?" I try changing the topic.

"Huh?" she questions.

"You should go spend some time with Daniel." I add. I don't know whether I am really acting weird or not, but I am happy and I can't contain the happiness inside me.

"Uh, he is watching some football game." She sighs.

"So, you should try and get his attention, maybe wear his favourite lingerie or something. I'll be locking myself up in the room." I mock her.

She makes a deadpan face and doesn't reply and walks out of the kitchen. I am midway eating my breakfast when I realize that I'd already promised Stella about going to the Prom with Eric, not only that but I've already asked him. SHIT! I immediately come to my room, with the bowl of corn flakes and check my phone. It is then I remembered that Jason had called me, yesterday in the evening when I was asleep. I recollect our conversation and feel like punching myself in the face. I decide to call Jason later on and instead call Eric.

"Hello," he answers.

"Are you free for a while, like an hour or so?" I question him, munching the leftover breakfast.

"Yes. Why?" he questions.

"If only I had to tell you everything over the phone, why would I ask you to meet up?" I say.

"Point to be noted," he replies.

"I'll come around four?" he adds.

"Okay," I sigh and hang up. I think of calling Jason or at least text him back, but I can't until I sort things out with Eric and Stella. I inform Susan and Daniel about Eric and we talk for a while about the wedding and the new school and Daniel's new venture, etc. I keep checking my phone every few minutes and keep playing with the locket in my neck. I keep framing sentences about how will I explain everything to Eric and Stella. It is quarter to four and I am too scared regarding the whole situation so I bring some cookies and ice cream from the kitchen. Eating helps me release the stress and I focus more on the food and how it tastes. The doorbell rings and Susan opens the door, Eric is three minutes and eight seconds early. He exchanges smile with Susan and Daniel and sits near me on the couch.

"We are going for a walk," Susan says, smiling.

"Come soon," I reply as they both get out of the house.

"So, what's going on?" Eric asks, curiously.

"Cookies?" I offer, passing the plate.

"Okay, please don't hate me after you hear what I've got to say?" I ask.

"Mmm-hmm," he replies, looking at the cookie in his hand. I close my eyes and pray in my mind that he understands everything and doesn't expect me to repeat it.

"Yesterday, at the wedding Jason asked me out for the Prom." I finally let it out, opening my eyes.

"So?" he questions, eating the cookie.

"So, I promised you that I would be going with you," I say.

"So?" he questions again, focused on the cookie.

"Eric!" I shout.

"What?" he shouts finally looking at me.

"I am talking to you." I say.

"Ohh, I am so sorry, I didn't know that. I know. I am listening." he explains.

"You are completely okay, with me going with him?" I question.

"Are you provoking me to throw a fit on that or something?" he says.

"No, why ... would ... I..." I run out of words.

"I don't know what to say," he replies.

"I can come with you if you want, I mean I'll talk it out with Jason, I am sure he'll understand," I explain.

"I really appreciate that, but I am happy and now that things are falling into place, I don't want to create any confusion between the two of you," he says.

"Sure?" I ask him again.

"Yeah and besides who wants to go to the Prom with you, look at you, you haven't taken a bath yet!" He mocks, laughing.

"That is so mean," I mutter under my teeth.

"Jason, just did me a favour and now that you are finally going with him, I am gonna ask Stella," he adds, laughing.

"Yeah, whatever," I reply, making a deadpan face.

"Haha...ha...ha." He laughs.

"I am just worried how Stella would react to this entire Jason thing," I say and he stops laughing.

"It depends," he says.

"I am sure she is going to be mad at me for a while and also she hates Jason." I add.

"Yeah, she sure does because Jason never tries to come into anybody's good-books except yours," he explains.

"I am so dead!" I sigh, imagining the entire situation. Stella is going to be a big pain-in-ass.

In the meanwhile, Susan and Daniel arrive and all of us chat for a little while until Eric leaves. I think of calling Stella but I don't think that it's the right time to explode the Jason bomb; I decide to wait because my Greek God is a little reckless and this Prom thing can be one of his mind games. I fidget with my cell phone, walking to my room and end up calling Dad.

"I wish you were here," Dad says, answering the call.

"If I was there, you two wouldn't be having the time of your life," I tease him.

"How is everything up there?" he questions.

"Perfect, Daniel has come and he'll be here until Christmas," I inform.

"You should call Eric over and have the time of your life," he teases me.

"He was here, a while ago," I reply.

"Ahh, things are going steady between the two of you," he adds.

"No, not really and to be precise I am just friends with him." I clarify.

"Well, he isn't. I've seen him blushing when you are around him," he says.

"Forget it, where is Jen?" I ask him.

"She's clicking the Eiffel tower," he informs.

"Honey, you should see the tower, its breathtakingly tall and beautiful," I hear Jen's voice.

"I'll plan a trip with Susan and Daniel or maybe the two of you," I reply.

"We miss you so much," she adds.

"I miss you more," I reply, smiling. I hear a beep voice in my ears and check my screen; Jason's call is on waiting.

"I'll call you in a while," I say.

"Yeah, love you, take care," Jen says.

I disconnect the call and stare at the screen for a few seconds, it displays, 2 missed calls Jason. My heart sinks a little, thinking what if he's changed his mind. What if he says, he can't go with me? At the same time my screen flashes again, Jason.

"Hello," I sigh, receiving his call.

"Hi," he whispers from the other end. His voice seems a little different today, just a little more mysterious.

"What's with your voice?" I ask him and regret it the moment these words slip out of my mouth. It's such a lame question and besides what he'll think about me.

"I was sleeping," he answers. Wow! I didn't expect him to really answer that, the unreasonable Jason never does, is he changing?

"Okay," I reply and then there is an awkward silence between us, the one that you're comfortable in.

"So, you have got anything important to say?" I ask him. I am not familiar with him calling me without holding any reason and also I want to know whether he has changed his mind.

"Uh... I don't think I need any reason to call the girl who I'll take to the Prom," he replies.

Now that makes me blush like heaven. I wish I could've recorded this entire conversation.

"Okay, it's just that I am too startled with this entire thing," I say, touching the chain on my neck.

"Well, then I guess you should prepare yourself, because there's a lot more to come," he says and I feel him smile.

"Like what?" I ask him.

"Don't you think you should let me keep doing the things that startle you?" he questions.

"It's not like startle, I kind of get a mini heart attack." I say.

"Then, Miss Casey Dalton, grab your heart tightly because tomorrow will be the best day of your life!" he announces.

"Okay," I manage to reply. My heart is already beating a little faster.

"I can't wait to see you tomorrow, take care," he adds.

"You too," I reply and the line cuts from the other end. I take a deep breath and smile remembering our conversation.

"Why are you smiling?" Susan questions me as I sit beside her.

"As if you don't know," I reply.

"Okay, so he hasn't changed his mind," she says, smiling.

"I am ordering dinner, what are you going to have?" Daniel questions me.

"Love," I reply, laughing.

"What?" he says, shocked.

"Nothing, pizza would be perfect," Susan orders.

******

We have the pizzas and grilled chicken wings; I can't eat more than two slices and just taste the wings. Once the dinner is over, I clean up the dishes and bid both of them goodnight, leaving them alone to spend some quality time together. Back in my room, I am smiling like an idiot and just then Jason texts me;

Good night.

Sweet dreams. I reply back immediately, blushing. All of this seems like a dream. I too can't wait to see him tomorrow; I hope I get some sleep tonight.

I hope he falls in love with me, the way I did. I've fallen in love with him; every part of him; good and bad and especially his flaws. I hope he falls in love with me; every part of me, although I can be whatever he wants me to be because lately my heart has become a, hopeless romantic.

******

"Wake up, Susan!" I shake her shoulders for the fifth time. Daniel is already up and has left for his morning walk, Susan is snuggled up in the blanket and I hardly got any sleep last night. I just kept tossing and twisting in the bed imagining the entire Prom night in different situations. It is in the morning I realize that I don't have anything appropriate to wear and I've heard earlier that lack of clothes is a huge crisis but today, around 6:55 a.m. I experienced that very moment. I've my entire wardrobe upside down, my room seems like a store on fifty percent discount; everything scattered around and my best friend Susan is busy snoring right now.

"Susan!" I shout in her ears.

"Stop shouting in my ears," she finally speaks, opening her eyes.

"Thank God!" I sigh in relief.

"Why are you acting so wild, lately?" she questions, tying her hair.

"Because I just realized, I've nothing to wear," I complain, making a depressed face.

"You know what Casey?" she mumbles.

"What?" I ask

"This Jason is turning you into a crazy creature!" she adds, walking to the wash room.

"Is it bad?" I ask, worried.

"No, no, it makes you more real. You speak a lot these days," she completes, banging the door on my face.

"That was mean, Susan!" I scream.

"And the way you wake me up in the morning is not mean?" she screams.

"I hate you!" I reply and walk to my room, thinking what I should wear. I think of calling Jen, she may help me out.

"Morning honey," she says, answering the call.

"Jen, there is a huge problem," I sigh.

"What, did you miss your periods!" she screams.

"Arrgghh! No, for Heaven's sake, just stop thinking all this nonsense!" I scream.

"Okay, sorry," she replies.

"I don't have anything to wear for the Prom and it's tonight, please just help me..." I beg.

"Ohh, I am so so sorry, I completely forgot to tell you," she says and pauses.

"What?" I interrupt.

"Just check out your Dad's closet, the last shelf. I've got a little something for you," she adds.

"Okay, I'll call you in five." I tell her and rush into Dad's room. I open the closet and see a box wrapped in pink, I immediately open it and...

"Whoa." Is the only thing that escapes my mouth. I take it out of the box, the dress is flawless. It is a dark peach or near red strapless dress; sweet heart neck covered under crystals all over the chest area, pleated empire waist and a layered chiffon skirt which would end around my thighs. Well, the dress is quite fascinating, but I don't know whether I'll be comfortable in this one and on top of that it is strapless. The last time I wore a strapless dress was at the wedding and all the time I was so conscious. Also, it has a built up bra inside which means I'll be more alert around Jason. I get myself into the dress and already feel half naked. I don't see myself in the mirror and rush to the room where Susan is.

"Ta-da!" I say, entering the room.

Susan gets off the bed and circles around me, watching me from top to toe and says,

"Dude, you look fucking hot!"

"Is that a compliment?" I question her, confused.

"If I were a boy, I'd do anything to get that dress off your body," she adds.

"What? Do I look slutty? I don't want to look slutty." I bargain.

"No, you look as tempting as Jason does," she says.

"Wait a second, a while ago you had nothing to wear and now you are all dolled up?" she questions.

"Well, I have a super surprising Mum" I reply, smiling.

"Uh-huh," she replies, making a face.

"And, get me another one like this." she adds, touching the fabric.

I am so delighted that I call up Jen and thank her a million times. Once, the dress is decided I spend two hours bathing in the tub, polishing myself. Jason, texts me in the afternoon that he would be picking me up around 7:00 p.m. and once I read the text I can't help myself from watching the time every five minutes. Susan paints my nails with the matching colour and curls up my hair into a messy look. She insists that I should wear a hairdo, but I am too nervous in that dress already. My loose hair would at least cover my shoulders and chest and save a lot of eyes in my direction. The entire afternoon passes in a jiffy and Daniel too can't believe that I am the same Casey he'd met a year ago. I keep imagining scenarios; about how would Stella react when she finds out about me and Jason and on top of that, one word keep bugging me a lot, Lyra. I don't know how she'd act and I thought of asking Jason about her over the phone but I just couldn't and it's better to discuss such things when he is with me, at least I can read his eyes then. Once the clock turns six, it really gets out of hand to wait for him. I keep looking at myself in the mirror again and again, making sure I don't look sluttish in anyway. The only thing I have on my body is that dress, the chain that Jason has gifted and matching ballet shoes. I practice walking in heels, but it is too difficult to balance and besides that I didn't want to create any mess today. I borrow a scarf from Susan, to keep myself covered and warm if things don't turn out the way I think; also it is cold outside and I don't want to sneeze right in the middle of the kiss.

Chapter 12

I take a deep breath, opening the door. He looks charming as always, wearing a white shirt, navy blue blazer over it and matching pants. My heart keeps skipping beats as he keeps looking at me like he has never seen me before. A moment later, he draws his reckless eyes in mine and whispers,

"I have half mind of not taking you to the Prom."

"Why?" I ask, immediately. My heart stops beating that very moment.

"Because, you look enchanting," he whispers and I can't resist a smile. Suddenly, I hear my heart beating like a drum. Embarrassed, I step a little aside.

"The entire day I've been practicing how to dance without hurting myself and now we are not going to the Prom," I sigh, walking forward to his car and leaning on it, partly.

"Aww..." he mimics, walking and leans beside me, a little too close. I look at him and his face is expressionless but I still consider myself lucky to have him beside me, close enough that I am able to differentiate the colour of his iris; where it turns to a lighter shade of emerald leaving the rest of it darker. I realize that we have been standing next to each other for a while now, so,

"I want to meet everyone, especially Stella and ... maybe your girlfriend; Lyra," I purposely bring her between us, now I know this spoils everything but hey, I need to know what's going on outside my world. I mean, I don't want to live in a bubble full of possibilities and with Jason, things are complex, always.

"Lyra?" he questions, all confused.

"Yes, your girlfriend." I answer, looking into his eyes.

"My girlfriend?" he questions again, his eyes playing around with mine.

"Yes Jason, your girlfriend Lyra." I say, stressing the word girlfriend and Lyra.

"Well, the only girlfriend I ever wish to have is a girl named, Casey," he replies, bringing his face a little more close. My cheeks turn all red and I try my best to hide what I feel.

"As far as I remember, you've a girlfriend and what's her name...umm...Lyra," I respond, hiding my smile, making a straight face.

"Okay, okay. I am not dating her anymore," he finally confesses.

"Uh-huh?" I doubt him. Well, it is obvious that they are not dating anymore, but you cannot beat Jason in these mind games.

"Yes, I ditched her the day I asked you out," he clarifies.

"What?" I say, a little shocked.

"You can't just break up..." I run out of words, getting confused within my own self.

"Why can't I break up?" he questions.

"Because... I don't know," I answer, looking away. I feel weird. I mean I should be screaming and dancing and happy knowing that Jason is all mine now, but I just feel awkward and weird and maybe sad.

"Hey!" I hear Susan's voice, out of nowhere. I lift my gaze upwards and she is standing at the door, clueless.

"Aren't you getting late for your Prom?" she shouts again.

"Yes," Jason replies, removing the keys from his pocket. He walks around and opens the door signalling me to get inside. I get into the car, still engrossed in my thoughts and watch him get in too. I still can't believe that he has broken up with her and now he is taking me to the Prom. No, I can't go to the Prom with him, not now. What am I supposed to explain to Stella and what if Lyra accuses me that I am the reason behind their break up? Wait a minute. Why did they break up in the first place? Is that really because of me?

"Why did you break up, with her?" I blurt it out.

"Now, where did that come from?" he questions, driving the car.

"I want to know, why did you break up, all of a sudden?" I insist.

"Because I wanted to," he replies.

"Why?" I shout at him, getting impatient.

"She cheated on me," he finally answers.

"So, that's the reason you are with me? Just because she cheated on you, it's not you who ditched her. Technically she ditched you," I mutter under my teeth, tears emerging in my eyes. I thought Jason did really love me and so he had broken up with her but I am a bloody option for him; just an option.

"Stop the car!" I scream, tears streaking down my face.

"Why?" he questions, yet driving the car.

"Because I am just an option for you," I answer in my broken voice.

"What makes you think that?" he questions, his voice getting a little sharper.

"You just told me that she cheated on you and so you ditched her, which means if she'd been loyal you wouldn't have asked me out, right?" I shout at him in my broken voice. I am hurt, real bad.

"God, you are crazy!" he screams

"Just stop the car," I order.

"I had been planning to get rid of her for quite a while and the day when I asked you out, I saw her with David. David is his ex-boyfriend," he pauses.

"And it was me who created a situation where David bumps into her and makes it look like she'd cheated on me," he completes.

"What?" I say, shocked.

"Yes, just because I get a real reason to break up and she tried a lot to convince me that she wasn't cheating on me but when I didn't believe her, she confessed about cheating on me with two other guys," he adds.

"That is it. And now if you want to walk away, you can," he says, stopping the car. I keep looking at him like a star struck fan.

"You actually did all of that?" I ask him again.

"Yes," he replies, starting the car.

"Does she know that you asked me out for the Prom?" I ask.

"I don't know," he replies.

"But then, we can't go to the Prom," I say, confused. Okay, so Lyra is indeed a bitch but I don't want a cat fight or something at the Prom and when I am already feeling too shy in this dress. I look around and see that it isn't the way to the venue.

"Jason, where are we going?" I ask him, looking around.

"Where ever this road takes us," he replies, smiling.

"This is so not fair," I complain, making a face. Suddenly, the car stops near the same church where we'd kissed for the first time. I get a little too upset thinking about that night and that Jason doesn't remember any of it. Turning my face towards him, I see him removing something from his blazer.

"For you, my lady, the love of my life," he says, pulling the rose out. I am tongue tied. How can he speak these words the same way exactly. He'd done the same thing that night when he was drunk. How is that possible? Maybe I am thinking too...

"I have something to confess." His voice interrupts my thoughts.

"I remember kissing you, that night," he adds.

"You remember?" I ask him shocked; my mind has completely stopped working now.

"Who wouldn't?" he says.

"I know I've been acting unreasonable all this while but I needed time to sort things out and now that I know what you mean to me, I am not letting you go anywhere, not now, never," he completes.

"Why didn't you tell me then? I thought you didn't remember any of that and also you acted all innocent in the class the next day," I reply.

"Yes I know, I should have told you but I wasn't sure how you would react. I did not want to hurt you then," he says.

"But you did hurt me," I say, tears emerging in my eyes.

"Stop crying, please," he murmurs, bringing himself closer.

"It's not fair; you kept me in the dark all this while," I complain.

"I kept you in the dark because I thought bringing you in the light would hurt you," he says, his fingers wiping the tears away, touching my cheeks.

"And now, it won't?" I complain,

"I don't know about that but I do know, each time something hurts you, I'll fix you back together, always," he says, placing the rose in my hand.

"But what's the guarantee that you wouldn't keep any secrets from me, or who knows, you're keeping right now or maybe..."

I try to frame a sentence, without losing myself in his eyes when he interrupts, "Now, if you keep blabbering, how am I supposed to kiss you?"

I sheepishly smile and reply, "You're changing the topic, smart ass."

"No, I am..." Before he completes, I plant a kiss on his lips.

"That's how you kiss when someone keeps blabbering stuff," I remark.

"Well, you're highly mistaken with the concept of kissing," he replies.

"No, how can I..."

Just as I try to complete my sentence, he cradles love over my lips. His hands, one intertwined into mine, tightly and the other, over my cheek. I pull out the other hand and touch his cheeks, softly. The moment I touch his face, I feel him smiling between the kiss. His grip over my hand tightens as the space between us contracts, expanding the space between our lips. We keep kissing each other, until our lungs get out of breath; his first. He distances his face only to meet my gaze, his hands still holding mine and my hand cupping his face. Our heartbeats synchronize with each other's; mine a little louder.

"Casey Dalton, I love you. I want to spend my life loving you because every time I see you, I see you differently. Every day, I discover something incredible within you. You and me, we just have that connection and that keeps drawing my soul towards yours. Be mine. My own little paradise, will you?" he whispers. Each word spoken through his soft lips, meant like prayer to my ears.

"Yours," I declare myself to him.

"I too have something to confess," I add, breathing heavily.

"I wasn't drunk that night when all of us went out for dinner; Eric had changed my drink with plain mineral water," I sheepishly confess.

"Okay and why did he do that?" he questions.

"Because, I was scared that maybe I would screw up things and openly tell you what I hold for you and besides, I have never been drunk in my entire life so, it seemed a great option." I explain.

"You have never been drunk?" he questions shocked.

"No, not like drunk, drunk. I've never got myself out of hand," I say remembering.

"Really?" he questions again.

I just nod thinking whether not getting drunk is a sin or something because the way he looks at me, makes me think it is.

"And, what about the dinosaur part?" he questions.

"Well, I was just pretending to be drunk." I say, smiling.

"How about not pretending now?" he asks.

"Let's get you drunk tonight!" he says, excited.

"I don't think that's a good idea, what if I go out of hand or do something incredibly crazy?" I say.

"Wherever you go, in the end you are going to fall in my arms," he says, kissing my forehead.

"Don't tell me later, that you regret it," I reply.

"I would never regret a moment spent under your presence, in fact I regret those that I don't," he responds, planting a peck on my lips.

He drives the car in the direction of his house and never leaves my hand for a second. I watch him driving the car, with a faint smile on his lips. I keep recalling the moment when he'd finally said those words, "Casey Dalton, I love you. I want to spend my life loving you because every time I see you, I see you differently. Every day, I discover something incredible within you. You and me, we just have that connection and that keeps drawing my soul towards yours. Be mine. My own little paradise, will you?" My heart is doing a happy dance knowing that, I AM HIS OWN LITTLE PARADISE!! He loves me as much as I love him. The guy who seemed completely out of my league is mine today; moreover I am dying to be his.

******

I wait for him, sitting on the couch feeling altogether different. I hold the scarf close enough to me because I am constantly getting goose bumps all over my body. Well, his house isn't decorated, just the same. I did expect a small Christmas tree at least. I see him walking with a dish holding eight tiny glasses or the shots.

"Ever tried tequila?" he questions, placing the dish on the table.

"No," I reply, confused and remembering whether I'd ever had.

"Try some, it's Christmas after all!" he says, picking one.

"And you are going to regret it." I say, picking for myself. We gulp all of it down, four each. A few minutes pass by and I feel different, I feel happier. It's like...

25th December, 2013

I open my eyes, as the sun kisses my face with light. I turn my face aside, twisting myself on the side and see my dream. I stroke his face with my fingers, smiling. He looks beautiful, the sun rays dancing on his face illuminating the bright red colour of his lips, his eyes closed and his breathing shallow. He is sleeping; his body half positioning facing mine, one of his hands is still around me forming a loose embrace. I look at him with sleep in my eyes; he is so subtle like Love. As I observe him, I see the rays of sun, playing around his lips, forming shadows. I immediately touch his soft lips with mine, envied by the rays. The moment I touch his lips, he moves a little and draws me closer to himself. As I snuggle inside him I feel him kissing my hair and also that there is nothing except this blanket over my body. I feel his skin against mine, so soft and full of warmth, under the soft blanket we'd been sharing since... I try to remember the previous night but my heavy eyes and the pain in my head wouldn't let me. Therefore, I close my eyes and let the memory of how we ended up naked together soak in...The first memory that flashes by, are empty glasses and then everything comes back to life.

"Feels good?" he questions.

"Yeah, I feel like I am flying," I reply, smiling like an idiot.

"We should have gone to the Prom; all my dance moves got wasted," I blabber.

"Well, I don't think so," he says, walking to the music player and tuning on a melody.

"May I?" he questions, offering his hand.

I hold his hand and he helps me get off the couch. We stand in the middle of the living room, our bodies moving around with the rhythm. I try recollecting the dance moves, but I just can't, instead I keep swinging around.

"Who...oops!" I say, losing my balance.

"Gotcha!" Jason says, helping me back on my feet.

"I love you," he murmurs.

"I love you," I whisper, looking in his eyes. He smiles and strokes my hair kissing me on my cheek.

"You don't celebrate Christmas?" I ask.

"Not really," he says, rolling his eyes. I smile not knowing whether it is the happiness and love that surrounds me or the tequila!

"But now, I do have a reason to celebrate," he says.

I am looking at the ceiling, trying to stop the fan that keeps moving round and round and round...

"Mr Claus sent me a gift, I never asked for but always wanted to," he adds, stroking my hair again.

"Tequila?" I ask him, still looking upwards.

"You," he whispers in my ears, bringing me closer, making me forget the ceiling and the fan.

His warm breath dances on my neck. I clench his arm, liking the feeling on my neck, as he pulls me a little closer, not that we are far from each other, but close enough for our bodies to touch, for our souls to connect. His soft fingers playing on and around my shoulders, slowly, separating the scarf from my body, as he keeps planting kisses on my neck, my ear and cheek. As his soft tender lips trace love on my neck, my body sets on fire. I experience a burning sensation all along and inside my body, every inch of skin ached for his touch. Finally, he drops the scarf on the floor and playfully runs his fingers over my naked shoulders and back. He brings his mouth close to mine and the cool air that escapes his lips tempts me to feel him, more than ever before. The way he seduces my skin, makes me gasp for more of him. I meet his eyes and they glow full with mischief, he is purposely making me long for his touch and, now that I know this, I can no longer wait for him to find my lips. Finally, I crash my lips into his, trying to absorb him as much as I can. He kisses me enough to stop the fire that burnt inside me, but only to enhance it again. His fingers tracing designs on my collar bone as he loses his breath and pulls his lips away, clamping his lower lip with his teeth,

"I love you," he whispers, touching my forehead with his and closes his eyes.

"I love you," I immediately whisper and his lips form a curve. He opens his eyes and they radiate the love he holds for me. He fondles my lower lip with his thumb and his touch, makes me feel like I am in heaven. Then his hand moves around, behind my head, his fingers making a way between my hairs and bringing my face closer he kisses me, furiously. The way he kisses me this time around, trembles my soul. I always knew he is reckless, but I didn't know that he wants me so much; that he burns for me as much as I do. He kisses my lower lip a little too much and softly clamps it with his teeth. I hold his face in my palm and that makes him realize that he has been kissing me a little too much.

He drinks me, to stop what is burning inside him but I know I am not enough; I will never be, because whatever is making him burn, it is making me burn too and maybe, just maybe, it is love and, it just grows with time, it never stops. After we exchange a few heartbeats, he lifts me up into his arms and climbs upstairs, not breaking the eye contact between us. As I hit my feet on the floor, I hear the melody of the song playing downstairs until our lips meet each other; then my ears are full with our heartbeats. His fingers reach to undress me as my hands reach to unbutton his shirt. It takes him a moment to slip the dress slowly down my body, pushing me softly on the bed yet kissing me intensely. I do not succeed enough to get him out of that shirt so, he helps me open it and I hear a few buttons rolling down the floor. After few more breathtakingly incredible kisses, he is all over me, his hands exploring every corner of my body; my soul as I surrender myself to him. I keep kissing him consistently all over, as he gets breathless. We rest together in the dimly lit room, the sound of our heartbeats synchronizing with the music in the background and his eyes fixed on me, our souls intertwined into each other makes me realize what heaven feels like. His hands tangled in my hairs and mine on his shoulder, keeping him close to myself, I read a series of emotions in his eyes; love, passion, concern, delight, happiness, desire and the sweet pain that made us one.

I was wounded soul, but he blew air over my wounds and they healed within a blink of an eye. He kissed my naked soul, leaving behind the love trapped on his lips and as he caressed my fragile soul with his soft hands, he left a few fingerprints here and there, giving me an altogether new identity; I felt like his possession because we leave a part of ourselves on the things we possess the most.

I see the time in the clock, on the side table; it is Christmas.

"Merry Christmas," I whisper to him, planting a kiss on his lips.

"Merry Christmas," he whispers kissing my forehead.

We lay next to each other, my head on his chest and his arm around me, my left leg on his, trying to side hug him and the blanket keeping us warmer. Words don't matter anymore, neither does the pace of his heartbeats, or the magic that surrounds us, all that matters to me is him and that, now he is a part of me, a part so precious that I'll sell my soul to keep him with me. I snuggle inside him, as I see him close his eyes, slowly.

******

I have a grin on my face as I recollect the memories and the same time he opens his eyes.

"Last night was the best night I'd ever had," he mumbles, blushing.

"Well, you are going to have a few more, maybe the rest of your life because I am not planning to leave you," I respond, kissing his nose.

"Never?" he questions, his eyes full with mischief.

"Never," I reply, smiling.

"Well, in that case, Miss Casey Dalton even if you wish to go away I am not going to let that happen," he pauses, twisting a little.

"Because I don't let people come near me unless I plan to keep them forever," he completes and brings his face closer to mine, resting his lips as I let him kiss me and just then we don't stop...

******

love

noun \ 'luhv \ pl.-s: a strong feeling of affection.

I Google the meaning of Love and it pretty much fails my expectations because what I hold for Jason is far beyond affection. For me, love means giving your heart to someone and trusting the one with it and that he would take care of it, like it's his own. It's like waking up every morning and finding him the reason to live for or thinking about him when you see a picture or hear a joke or see his favourite colour. Its 11:11 p.m. And you don't make a wish for yourself, instead you wish for him because that smile on his face means everything to you. Love is wearing the clothes he likes even when you don't or doing everything that makes him happy; play a video game or something so that you get to spend time with him or remembering how much milk he pours in his coffee. It's fighting like animals and ending up kissing each other midway or just holding hands while walking on the street or the silent moments that the eyes exchange. Love is how just his presence calms your mind or how his mood swings affect you; like when he is upset you're upset too and how his smile makes you smile even when you're at your worse. It's as simple as watching him sleep and making sure that you don't wake him up and as complicated as seeing him talking, just talking to any random girl and how you get jealous, automatically. Love is to let him explore into your soul, because as much as it's yours, it's his too and so are the scars and wounds on it. Love is innocent and pure. Love has no logic or reasoning. Love is selfless. Love is calm. Love is fierce. Love is full of desires. Love is unconditional. Love is priceless. Love is eternal. Love is him.

And to love isn't easy, love anyway.

www.ingramcontent.com/pod-product-compliance
Lightning Source LLC
Chambersburg PA
CBHW032002170626
46807CB00006B/2609